Stark's
Justice

James Reasoner

Stark's Justice

WHEELER
PUBLISHING, INC.

★ AN AMERICAN COMPANY ★

Published in Large Print by arrangement with Pocket Books in the United States and Canada.

Wheeler Large Print Book Series.

Set in 16 pt. Plantin.

Library of Congress Cataloging-in-Publication Data

Reasoner, James.
  Stark's justice / James Reasoner.
    p. (large print) cm.—(Wheeler large print book series)
  ISBN 1-56895-153-1
  1. Large type books. I. Title. II. Series.
  [PS3568.E2685S73 1994]
  813'.54—dc20   94-35471
                                                         CIP

For the rest of the Jackson Hole Gang:

Doug Grad of Pocket Books
Paul Block and Pam Lappies,
     ridin' for that BCI brand
My good friends Bill and Judy Crider
My dad, Marion Reasoner

And for Livia, who made me go up there in the first place and held down the fort while I was gone . . .

This book wouldn't have been written without them.

Big Earl says thanks.

Prologue

". . . The voice of frontier justice had its origins in many different locales and personifications: the trail boss, settling disputes around a lonely cow camp fire; the sky pilot, taking for his example the wisdom of Solomon as he counsels his flock and steers them onto the proper path; the newspapermen with their fiery editorials, leading by example; the peace officers, seeking to bring order and reason to a land traditionally governed by disorder and unreason; the legislators, codifying the rules by which man shall live and govern himself; and the lawyers themselves, bringing those rules to the common man and leading him through the forests of confusion and into the clearing of understanding.

"These and many others contributed mightily to the formation of the legal system as it is practiced and carried out today in that vast and glorious area known as the American West. Not for us the stuffy attitudes so often to be found in our esteemed colleagues who practice their profession to the east of the mighty Father of Waters. The West is its own place, with its own problems and solutions, and justice out here is a fluid thing, ever changing, open to the opinions of the many rather than the few. In the West, every man counts, and so does what he believes. And the law must take that into account, because who knows

1

from what source the telling point will come. It might as well originate in the sage words of a grizzled old-timer as in the more polished oratory of a member of the bar. It is especially vital for a jurist to remember these things and not close his ears to wisdom just because it may not be couched in the flowery, high-flown language all too common to our courts these days. A judge himself should always remember his own past, recall the place and the time from which he himself sprang.

"It is important to remember that I never set out to be a judge, or even an attorney. My life had followed another course entirely until it reached a certain point, and whether its turning was mere happenstance or the mysterious workings of Fate, none, least of all myself, can say. One thing, however, is certain: it all began on a blustery day in the rugged frontier community of Buffalo Flat . . ."

—Excerpt from transcript of an address given by Judge Earl Stark at the annual meeting of the Western United States Bar Association, Denver, Colorado, August 1, 1895

Chapter One

The stagecoach was about an hour behind schedule as it rolled into Buffalo Flat, a frontier town in the southwestern part of Texas. The manager of the community's stage station, who also happened to be the owner and operator of the line, was waiting impatiently on the porch of the building as the jehu brought the big red-and-yellow-painted Concord to a stop that left the coach rocking slightly on its leather thoroughbraces.

"What happened, Billy?" the stage line owner asked anxiously as he stepped up to the coach and rested a hand on the box.

"Rear axle cracked, Mr. Suggins," replied the driver. "Happened when we hit that bad dip about four miles out, just this side of the gap. Earl an' me wired it up so's we could go on, but we had to take it mighty slow in places."

Suggins let out a groan at the news. He was a slender, sallow man wearing a vest, string tie, and sleeve garters on his white shirt. He ran a hand through his thinning hair and said in exasperation, "I suppose the axle will have to be replaced before you continue the run."

"I reckon so," Billy said. "The one that's on

3

there ain't goin' to hold up all the way to Fisherton."

Suggins nodded in grudging acceptance. "All right, pull the coach on around to the barn out back. We'll get started replacing the axle right away. With any luck, you won't lose more than another couple of hours."

As the driver nodded and lifted the reins, ready to get the team of eight horses moving again, the shotgun guard who sat beside him on the box raised a hand, saying, "Hold on there, Billy. No need for me to ride around back with you. I'll get off right here."

The driver paused, and the guard hopped down from the box, landing lighter on his feet than might have been expected from a man of his bulk. He was only of medium height, but he carried considerable weight on his burly frame. There was nothing soft about him, though, despite his size. He wore a tan duster and a broad-brimmed Stetson of the same color, both items covered with dust from the trail. Under the long coat were a leather vest and an old, faded blue cavalry shirt. A colorful bandanna was looped around the guard's neck, underneath the thick growth of dark beard shot through with gray. His brown eyes had the near-permanent squint of a man who had spent most of his life outdoors.

The guard was well armed, given his profession, not much of a surprise. He carried a shotgun—a greener with the barrels cut off a couple of inches shorter than they had come from

4

the factory, so that the scattergun would be a little easier to handle in close quarters—and riding in a well-worn holster on his right hip was a First Model LeMat two-barrel revolver with checkered walnut grips and the usual swivel lanyard ring set into the butt. The LeMat was a unique weapon, firing standard .42 caliber cartridges from its upper barrel, with the lower barrel accommodating a .63 caliber shotgun shell. The invention of Dr. Jean LeMat of New Orleans, it was known variously as the "Grape Shot Revolver" and the "Streetsweeper." Carried by some Confederate officers during the Late Unpleasantness, it was used mostly by lawmen now, who could cut down most of a mob with the shotgun barrel and then pick off the leavings with the regular slugs. Not noted for its accuracy, the LeMat was still one hell of a deadly weapon at close range.

It looked right at home on the hip of the burly shotgun guard.

"You'll be back in time to leave when the stage is repaired, won't you?" asked Suggins, sounding somewhat irritated as the guard turned toward the saloons that lined both sides of Buffalo Flat's main street.

"Sure, I'll be here, Martin. Don't worry 'bout that."

Suggins was still frowning slightly as the guard strolled off, but the big man didn't pay any attention to him.

It was an overcast day, with a cool wind whipping thick gray clouds through the sky. There

5

hadn't been any rain in these parts in quite a while, though, so the dust on the trail had been thick, the kind of dust that built up a good thirst in a man. The guard intended to quench that thirst in the first drinking establishment he came to.

Before he could reach the saloons, however, a commotion down the street caught his attention. The citizens of Buffalo Flat seemed to be converging on one saloon in particular, the Tumbling Dice. The pair of giant wooden dice that gave the place its name hung from the awning over the boardwalk in front of the batwing doors. The bearded man had been to the Tumbling Dice before, and the beer they served there was as cold and as good as any in Buffalo Flat. Might as well do his drinking there and see what in blazes was going on, he decided.

There was a crowd on the boardwalk with more people joining it all the time. With the greener tucked under his arm, the shotgun guard strolled toward the saloon, and when he was nearly there, he asked one of the men hurrying by, "What's all this uproar about?"

The man hesitated only a moment, just long enough to give the guard a look as if he couldn't believe anyone would ask such a foolish question. "Hell, haven't you heard?" the townie demanded. "They got Jed Stockdale on trial for murder! Judge Buchanan's closed the bar in the Dice and he's holdin' court in there, since we ain't got that new courthouse built yet."

The guard lifted an eyebrow in surprise as his informant rushed on toward the saloon. A light of excitement and curiosity began to shine in the big man's eyes. Matters of the law held a special interest for him, enough to make him forget his thirst. Nobody around here knew about it, but some months earlier a passenger had left a set of law books on one of the stages being guarded by the bearded man. He had latched on to them, unable to say why at the time, but since then he had been reading the books, studying them every spare moment he had, caught up in the spell of the words and concepts.

Here was a chance for a little practical education in the law, he decided. A chance to observe a real trial.

The guard pushed his way through the crowd around the batwings, his size and strength making that easy. The few angry looks and curses he drew in the process quickly subsided when folks looked around and saw who he was, recognizing him and the scattergun he carried under his arm. In a matter of moments he had reached the entrance of the saloon and slipped inside.

The long barroom was just as packed as the boardwalk outside. Men were standing shoulder to shoulder, craning their necks to see over the gents in front of them. The lucky ones had climbed on tables and towered over their neighbors. The only open space in the room was an area in front of the polished hardwood bar. Three of the tables normally used for poker, faro, three-card monte, and the like had been commandeered for the trial, which was just getting under way. One of the tables was placed near the bar for the judge, while the other two faced it side by side.

The state district court judge, Artemus Buchanan, was a middle-aged man with the face of a bulldog and a dusty black suit and beaver hat. His red nose and cheeks and slightly unfocused eyes testified that he had liberally sampled some of the bar's wares before shutting it down for the duration of the trial.

The guard got the back of his shoulders against the wall just inside the door of the saloon and settled down to listen as Buchanan used a bung starter to hammer on the table until the room quieted down. That took a while, because every one of the dozens of men inside the saloon seemed to have an opinion on the case and were presenting their arguments at the top of their lungs, including the twelve men in a row of straight-backed chairs who were evidently serving as the jury. They were a mixture of townsmen, farmers, and ranch hands. Finally, the place calmed down, and with a clatter the judge tossed his makeshift gavel onto the table in front of him.

"Goddammit, we're goin' to have order in this here courtroom!" Buchanan bellowed. "Anybody who opens his yap again without my say-so'll spend a night in the hoosegow!" That said, the distinguished jurist squared his shoulders, shot the frayed cuffs of his white linen shirt, belched loudly, and glowered at the prosecutor. "I reckon we're ready, Hamilton. Get 'er goin'."

The man called Hamilton got to his feet and rested the tips of long slender fingers on the prosecutor's table. "Thank you, Your Honor," he declared in the deep, mellifluous voice of a born orator. "And thank you as well for establishing at the outset the dignity and decorum that a proceeding such as this one so richly deserves."

Judge Buchanan put his left elbow on the table, rested his chin on the palm of his left hand, and waved his right to cut short the speechifying and hurry the prosecutor along.

"We have come here today," Hamilton began as he stepped around his table, "to see that justice is done! For a foul deed has been committed in our fair community, Judge, a deed so heinous and despicable that it literally cries out for redress! I am speaking, Your Honor, of—" and with that he spun around nimbly to face the audience crowding into the saloon as he intoned, "—murder!"

The shotgun guard's eyes narrowed slightly as he leaned against the wall and watched the goings-on. He recognized the gent running off at the mouth as the Right Honorable Cassius P. Hamilton, known throughout the territory as a congressional representative, attorney, and sometimes, when the legislature wasn't in session in Washington City, special prosecutor in his hometown of Buffalo Flat. Tall and slender, with his expensive cutaway coat, his impressive mane of dark gray hair, his neat goatee, and a speaking voice that had been known to deafen prairie dogs, Hamilton was the very picture of an oily, somewhat shady career politician—which was exactly what he was. He was also the most long-winded son of a bitch west of the Missisipp', the guard recalled from Fourth of July celebrations in the past, so it looked like it might take a while to get to the meat of this trial.

In the meantime, while Hamilton was going on about how horrible a crime murder was, dividing his histrionics equally between the judge, the jury, and the spectators, the shotgun guard turned his attention to the man sitting alone at the defense table. Evidently no one was representing him. It came as no surprise to the guard that the defendant was going to have to represent himself. Jed Stockdale might have one of the biggest spreads in the territory, but nobody around Buffalo Flat liked him, especially the small ranchers and the sodbusters. Stockdale was one of the old-time cattle barons who regarded neighboring ranchers with less than ten thousand head as a nuisance and farmers with their "dadblasted bobwire" as an annoyance. He'd run roughshod over the area for nigh onto thirty years, and now that he was on the defensive for once, the spectators in this makeshift courtroom seemed to be taking great pleasure in his discomfort.

Hamilton must have a mighty strong case against Stockdale, though, mused the shotgun guard, for none of the town's lawyers to take the job of defending him. Just from the looks of the trial's opening, a conviction seemed to be a foregone conclusion. The expression on Stockdale's leathery, whiskered face seemed to indicate that he felt the same way. The old man was a fighter, but he realized the deck was stacked against him.

"The prosecution shall show, Your Honor, that this man—" Hamilton leveled an accusing finger at Stockdale "—did knowingly, willfully, and maliciously bring to an end the life of his neighbor Herman Jeffords. Yes, this man, Jedediah Stockdale, committed that most awful and reprehensible of crimes." The special prosecutor let his voice drop and quiver with the rage he was expressing on behalf of the community. "He is a *murderer*."

Leaning over, the shotgun guard said quietly to the man standing beside him, "Ol' Cassius don't care much for Stockdale, does he?"

"Why should he?" replied the spectator. "Stockdale's had things his own way around here for so long he thinks he can get away with anything. It's damn well time somebody caught up to him and made him toe the line, and Hamilton's just the man to do it!"

The guard saw Hamilton glance toward them and knew that the prosecutor had somehow picked up the spectator's comment. A tiny smile tugged at Hamilton's wide mouth for a fraction of a second. He was putting on a show and he knew it, the guard thought. Hamilton wasn't much ashamed of the fact, either.

11

Convicting a man like Stockdale of murder would be quite a feather in Hamilton's cap and would make the politician even more well-known. That was like food and drink to Hamilton.

The opening argument was finally winding down, or maybe Hamilton was just running out of breath, as unlikely as that was. At last he made a closing flourish with his hand and said, "Thank you, Your Honor."

Judge Buchanan let out a loud snore.

Hamilton gave a discreet cough, and the judge awakened with a start and turned to Stockdale. "You got anything to say for openers?" Buchanan asked.

Stolidly, the grizzled rancher shook his head.

The judge sighed and looked back at Hamilton. "Call your first witness," he instructed.

"I shall be happy to oblige, Your Honor," Hamilton said as he sprang back to his feet, having sat down only seconds earlier. "The prosecution calls Calvin Jeffords, the poor, grieving brother of the murdered man!"

A pale-haired sodbuster in a new suit stepped forward from the crowd. The clothing was expensive, though it didn't fit him very well, and the shotgun guard supposed that Hamilton had bought the suit for his star witness. The man cast a nervous glance toward the judge and the jury, then sat down in the chair that the judge shoved toward him with a foot. Buchanan slid a Bible across the table and growled, "Put your hand on that."

Jeffords did as he was told, promising at the judge's prompting to tell the truth, the whole truth, and nothing but the truth, so help him God, before settling back in the chair and commencing to twist the shapeless black hat in his hands. He swallowed hard as Hamilton paced back and forth in front of him for a moment like a restless mountain lion.

"Now, Mr. Jeffords," Hamilton said, "tell us, if you will be so kind, what happened between your brother, the late Herman Jeffords, and the defendant in this case, Mr. Jedediah Stockdale."

"Well . . ." Jeffords began, then paused as his voice cracked a little. "They didn't get along, Mr. Hamilton, they didn't get along at all."

Hamilton clasped his hands together behind his back and regarded the witness with a hooded stare. "By that, do you mean they were not friends, Mr. Jeffords?"

"No, they weren't friends, not hardly. Herman couldn't stand Stockdale's guts, and I reckon the feelin' was mutual."

"You and your brother are farmers, are you not? Or rather, you are a farmer and your brother was one as well before his untimely, unjustified demise, is that correct?"

"Yes, sir. Herman and me, we got us a nice little place when we come out here a few years back. Raised some crops and some hogs and chickens and ran a few sheep and milk cows."

"And where is your farm located in relation to Mr. Stockdale's Ladder S ranch?"

13

"Our land sort of backs up to his, up along the northwest corner of his spread."

"So you're neighbors?" Hamilton asked with a patently phony smile.

"Our land's next to his," Jeffords replied. "I wouldn't say we was neighbors. Leastways, Stockdale was never very neighborly. Why . . . why, we hadn't been there a week when Stockdale and some of his hands rode up to our place and he told us we was goin' to have to get rid of them stinkin' sheep. That's what he called 'em, stinkin' sheep. Said he wouldn't have a bunch of damned woolies anywhere within a hundred miles of his range!"

The sodbuster's voice rose as he warmed to his subject, and beads of sweat popped out on his forehead even though the day was cool. His angry response prompted a murmur of comment in the makeshift courtroom, and Hamilton wisely let it run its course before asking his next question.

"How did you and your brother come to hold title to your land, Mr. Jeffords?"

"We worked, saved our money, and bought the place. How else would an honest man get hold of land?"

"How else indeed?" Hamilton asked, casting a meaningful glance at Stockdale. "In the past, some men took their land with the gun and the knife and the rope, and they think they can still hold it that way, despite the fact that the rule of law has come at long last into the West!"

14

Stockdale flushed angrily, but he didn't say anything. When he had come to this country, the town of Buffalo Flat had not existed, was not yet even a gleam in the eye of some land developer. The land had been there for the taking, for any man strong enough to hold it. For years Stockdale had been strong enough. But now the rules had changed. Sheep and barbed wire and men like Cassius P. Hamilton had changed them.

The shotgun guard knew all that, knew what had to be going through the rancher's mind. But Stockdale still sat quietly, his gnarled, callused hands sometimes clenching into fists for a few seconds at a time.

"What was the response of you and your brother when Mr. Stockdale told you to get rid of your sheep?"

"We told him we couldn't afford to do that, and that the land was ours and we'd do what we pleased with it."

"And what did Mr. Stockdale do then?"

"He told us he'd be seein' us again, said it real mean-like. Then him and his hands rode off . . . right through the garden Herman and me had just put in! Tore it up good, they did."

"I see. And that was just the beginning of the trouble between the two of you and Mr. Stockdale, was it not?"

"That's right. We didn't have nothin' but bad luck for months after that. Our crops caught fire and our milk cows got run off, and somebody shot our best sow and dumped the body in our well. More'n once, somebody took a shot at us, too. Came close to killin' us."

"And who do you suppose might have done those things, Mr. Jeffords?"

"I know damn well who did 'em! It was Stockdale and those no-good gunnies he calls ranch hands!"

Jeffords was on his feet now, yelling and pointing at the old rancher, who leaned back in his chair and fixed the witness with a cold, stony glare. Some of the spectators followed the lead of Jeffords and shouted their pent-up anger at Stockdale. Judge Buchanan picked up the bung starter and hammered it on the table again, and eventually the commotion died down.

"I warned you people," Buchanan said, pointing his finger at the spectators and motioning for Jeffords to sit down with a curt gesture of the bung starter. "I won't warn you again. Now get on with it, Hamilton, and for God's sake, try not to stir things up so much."

"With all due respect, Your Honor, I am only attempting to establish the truth for the gentlemen of the jury and the other good citizens of Buffalo Flat, so that they can see for themselves what sort of viper has long been lurking in the bosom of our community!"

Ignoring the judge's glare, Hamilton turned back to the witness. "And how long did this pattern of hostility on the part of Mr. Stockdale continue?"

"Right up until the end. Right up until that fight he had with Herman."

"Do you mean that blows were exchanged?"

"Hell, yes, blows were exchanged! It was right out there in the middle of Main Street. I reckon two dozen people must've seen Stockdale jump Herman and beat the hell out of him."

Again the spectators called their agreement, but they hushed rapidly when Buchanan reached for the bung starter.

"What happened then?" Hamilton asked quietly.

"I . . . I took Herman home and patched him up as best I could. He was ragin' like a mad dog, so mad at Stockdale that he couldn't hardly see straight. He said he was goin' to get his gun and ride over to Stockdale's ranch. Said he was goin' to settle things once and for all between 'em!"

"So, given the state of your brother's rage, is it likely that he did indeed attack Mr. Stockdale? Is it possible that Mr. Stockdale can plead self-defense in the killing of Herman Jeffords?"

With tears shining in his eyes, Calvin Jeffords shook his head. "No, sir, that ain't possible. Because Herman never went over there all mad like that. I calmed him down, told him it was time we put a stop to all the trouble. I told him that it wasn't worth it to keep runnin' those sheep."

"And your brother accepted that argument?"

"He did. We sold our sheep, ever' last one of

17

'em. Sold 'em to Leroy Parsons, who's got a place down south of here. He can tell you."

"We believe you, Mr. Jeffords, we believe you. Once you and your brother had disposed of your sheep, what did you do then?"

Jeffords took a deep breath. "Well, I didn't do anything. But Herman, he wanted Stockdale to know what we'd done. He saddled up and rode over there, said he was goin' to tell Stockdale he'd won." Again Jeffords swallowed hard. "That was the last time I seen my brother. He never came back, and I never seen him again, from that day to this!"

"And what do you suppose happened to your brother, Mr. Jeffords?" Hamilton asked softly. "Why do you think he never came back to your farm?"

"Because Stockdale killed him!" Jeffords was on his feet again, unable to control himself. "He killed poor Herman and had his hands throw the body in a ravine somewhere or bury it! You go look around the Ladder S! You'll find poor Herman's body there somewhere!"

Hamilton turned to the judge and cleared his throat. Reluctantly, Buchanan took his eyes off the pretty young woman among the spectators at whom he had been staring. Hamilton said, "The sheriff has conducted a search, Your Honor, but so far the body of the unfortunate Herman Jeffords has not been located. However, the Ladder S is a very large ranch, and there is more than enough evidence to prove that Jedediah

18

Stockdale killed Mr. Jeffords and had the body disposed of."

Swinging toward the jury, Hamilton began ticking off points on his fingers. "Consider the longstanding enmity between Mr. Stockdale and the Jeffords brothers. Consider the brutal beating that Mr. Stockdale administered to Herman Jeffords, right outside in the main thoroughfare of our community. Consider the capitulation on the part of Herman and Calvin Jeffords, the bowing to the unreasonable demands of Mr. Stockdale. You've heard the testimony, gentlemen. I could call further witnesses to give additional testimony about the hostile relationship between the defendant and the Jeffords brothers. But what would be the point? You have heard the story from the most reliable witness of all, Calvin Jeffords himself. You have heard how Herman Jeffords rode to the Ladder S and never returned. Ask yourself this question: What could have happened to Herman Jeffords? He was ready to put this feud behind him, ready to get on with the business of running the farm with his brother. But he *never returned*. What could have kept him away?" Hamilton paused dramatically for a moment, then said, "You know the answer to that as well as I do, gentlemen. *Death* is the only thing that could have kept Herman Jeffords from returning to his home. Death at the hands of Jedediah Stockdale!"

The prosecutor's voice thundered, making the silence that fell over the courtroom that much

19

more pronounced. In a voice little more than a whisper, Hamilton said, "No further questions, Your Honor. The prosecution rests."

Everyone in the place seemed to take a deep breath. Judge Buchanan looked at Jed Stockdale and asked, "Do you have any questions for this witness?"

"No need," Stockdale muttered. "He'd just lie some more anyway."

Jeffords started to say something, but Buchanan motioned for him to be quiet. "That's all," the judge said. "You can get out of the witness chair now."

Jeffords stood up and walked past the prosecution table. Hamilton patted him on the arm, then hooked his thumbs in his vest and looked over smugly at Stockdale.

"It's up to you, Stockdale," Buchanan told the old rancher. "What have you got to say in your own defense?"

"Nothin'," snapped Stockdale. "Nothin' except that it's a pack o' lies. I reckon I fussed a mite with them two sheepherders, but I didn't jump Herman that day in the street. He was a hotheaded bastard, and he's the one threw a punch at me. I just shoved him away, and he tripped over his own two feet."

Hamilton smiled indulgently, as if what Stockdale was saying was pathetically unbelievable.

"I didn't kill him, neither," Stockdale went on. "He may've started out ridin' toward my ranch, but he never got there. I never saw Herman Jeffords on the day he disappeared, and I didn't kill him." He crossed his arms, looked around the room defiantly, and concluded, "That's all I got to say. You can believe it or not, whatever you've a mind to. Can't say as I give a damn either way."

Standing near the doorway, the shotgun guard narrowed his eyes and frowned in concentration. Something was mighty wrong here. Stockdale might not realize just how much trouble he was really in. If the jury found him guilty of murder—and there wasn't much doubt that would be the verdict—the judge wouldn't have any choice except to sentence him to hang. And in that case, the sentence would likely be carried out right away, or as soon as a rope could be thrown over a limb of the nearest tree. Stockdale could be kicking his life away in a matter of minutes.

Judge Buchanan leaned forward and stared hard at Stockdale. "That's it? The only defense you've got is saying that you didn't do it?"

Stockdale shrugged. "I could make some of my boys lie for me, I suppose, and say they was with me all that day, but it ain't the truth. I was alone at the ranch house when Jeffords is supposed to have come over there." He swiped a hand across his face, the only visible sign of the tension he had to be under. "I gave my crew orders to stay away from town today and not to bother folks, no matter how this turns out. You

21

see, Judge, I've lived by my word for better'n fifty years. It's either good enough now or it ain't."

It wasn't going to be good enough this time, the burly guard sensed. This crowd was thirsty for blood and ready for a hanging, ready to see the top dog cut down at last.

The judge sighed and turned to the jury. "All right, you boys can withdraw for your deliberations. Just go in the back room there—"

The juryman at one end of the row stood up abruptly and shook his head. He exchanged a glance with his fellow jury members and got nods from all of them. Facing the judge again, he began, "We won't need no deliberations, Your Honor—"

This had gone on long enough, the shotgun guard decided. Shouldering aside the men between him and the open area where the trial was taking place, he stepped forward and boomed, "You sure as hell won't, 'cause this ain't no legal trial in the first place."

The saloon erupted with angry shouts and questions as everyone looked around to see who had dared to interrupt the grim festivities. The yelling was so loud and hostile, completely drowning out Buchanan's pounding of the bung starter, that the guard was tempted to touch off one barrel of the greener into the ceiling, just to shut everybody up. He reined in the impulse, though. He didn't want any gunplay in here unless it couldn't be avoided.

Finally, through a combination of the judge's

shouting for order and the guard's glowering at the angry men surrounding him, the uproar began to slacken. When at last it was quiet enough for the judge to be heard again, Buchanan stared incredulously at the shotgun guard and said furiously, "You look familiar, mister. Who in blazes are you?"

"Name's Earl Stark. They sometimes call me Big Earl."

The coolly voiced reply quieted the crowd even more. Those in the room who hadn't recognized Stark knew his name. Big Earl was the best-known shotgun guard in the whole territory, maybe the most feared in the whole West. Outlaws seldom dared to try holding up a stagecoach with him riding shotgun. The ones who were foolish enough to attempt it were usually cut down like so much wheat before a scythe by the greener Stark wielded with such deadly efficiency. He had no idea how many outlaws he had killed; he wasn't the sort of man to keep track of such things. All he knew was that when he was on a stage, the mail pouch, the express box, and the passengers always got where they were going and got there safely.

Buchanan was obviously aware of Stark's reputation, too, because he was somewhat less belligerent as he asked, "Just what makes you say this isn't a legal trial, Stark? We got a judge and a jury and witnesses."

"Where's the body?"

"What body?" asked Buchanan, frowning.

23

"That fella Herman Jeffords. The man who's supposed to be dead."

"He *is* dead!" Calvin Jeffords responded. "Why else wouldn't he come back to the farm?"

Stark shook his head. "Can't say as to that. But you can't try a man for murder if you can't find the body. They call it habeas corpus. You got to have a corpse on hand 'fore you can charge anybody with the killing."

Cassius P. Hamilton was on his feet, and his lip lifted in a sneer as he looked at the bearded man in dusty trail clothes. "You'll pardon me, sir," he said with arrogant mock politeness, "if I don't take the word of an individual such as yourself on a complicated legal point. I think I know a bit more about the law than you, Mr. Stark."

"It don't look like it from where I stand," Stark replied curtly. He looked at the judge again and went on, "If you've got a copy of Blackstone's *Commentaries* handy, Your Honor, you can look it up for yourself. Or I'll find it for you, if you like."

"No, that won't be necessary," Buchanan said hastily. "I'm, ah, familiar with the concept of habeas corpus, of course."

Hamilton stared at Stark, his eyes narrowed with dislike. "Blackstone," he repeated. "How is it that a shotgun guard knows so much about Blackstone and the law?"

"I been studyin' up on it," Stark replied. "And I know enough to see that you folks are tryin' to rail-road this jasper."

The special prosecutor was still sneering. "I take it, then, that you have some *other* explanation for the disappearance of Herman Jeffords? Perhaps you would care to represent Mr. Stockdale?"

Stark glanced at the old rancher, who had the gleam of hope in his eyes for the first time during this trial. Stockdale said, "I'll pay you, Stark—"

The big man shook his head abruptly. "I didn't speak up for money. Just wanted to see justice done. It's only common sense—if there's no corpse, how can anybody be sure there's been a murder done?"

Hamilton was about to make another sarcastic reply when several shouts suddenly sounded at the saloon's entrance. Everyone in the room swung toward the door, anxious to see what was going to happen next, but no one was prepared for the sight of the short, slender man who pushed through the crowd. His clothes were dirty and torn, his thinning brown hair in disarray. But he was so angry that the thick mustache over his mouth was almost bristling with fury. One of the bystanders behind him yelled in amazement, "Herman Jeffords!"

The supposedly dead man aimed a trembling finger at someone across the room and cried, "Damn you, Calvin!"

Heads snapped around again as the gazes of the enthralled spectators switched back to Calvin Jeffords, who had just testified that his brother

25

was dead, murdered by Jed Stockdale. Calvin's face was pale and contorted with surprise and anger, and his hand suddenly darted toward the butt of a gun holstered on the hip of a man standing beside him.

Stark acted instinctively, knowing he was the only one close to Calvin with his wits about him enough to do anything. He lashed out with his greener, its double barrels thudding against Calvin's skull. Calvin staggered, and the barrel of the gun he had just plucked from the other man's holster sagged toward the floor. Several men grabbed him and wrestled the pistol away from him.

"What's goin' on here?" Herman Jeffords demanded. "I come lookin' for help, and the whole damn town's havin' some sort o' party in a saloon!"

"This is no party!" Hamilton replied, sounding offended. "This is a court of law! And what are you doing alive?"

"I been alive all along, sittin' down there in that root cellar of our'n, after Calvin hit me on the head and tied me up! That no-good skunk thought with me out o' the way, he'd have the whole farm for hisself! Even bragged to me about it, he did. Said he was goin' to lay the blame for my killin' on ol' Jed Stockdale and get rid o' *him*, too." Herman sniffed disgustedly as he looked at his brother struggling futilely in the grip of the men who held him. "Only reason he ain't butchered me like a hog 'fore now is I wouldn't tell

26

him where I hid the money I got for sellin' all them sheep to Leroy Parsons. He said he'd starve it out o' me if he had to. I'd still be there if I hadn't managed to wiggle out o' the ropes he tied me up with and bust out the door o' the root cellar."

Hamilton was staring at Herman Jeffords, eyes wide and mouth working a little in astonishment as the story of Calvin's villainy unfolded. Nearly everybody in the room was babbling at the unexpected turn of events.

Earl Stark looked at Hamilton and said dryly over the hubbub, "I'm just a shotgun guard, Mr. Prosecutor, but it looks to me like you ought to move for a dismissal of all charges against Jed Stockdale and throw Calvin Jeffords in jail instead. Of course, that's just a suggestion from somebody who don't know much about the law."

After swallowing hard a couple of times, Hamilton nodded ruefully and motioned for quiet. To Buchanan he said, "I . . . I move for dismissal of this case, Your Honor."

"Granted," Buchanan agreed with a rap of the bung starter. "Best have the sheriff take Calvin Jeffords over to the jail, Mr. Hamilton."

Hamilton motioned for the lawman to carry out the order, and as Calvin was led away, the proprietor of the Tumbling Dice leaned over to Buchanan and said something in the judge's ear. Buchanan nodded, hit the table with the bung starter one last time, and announced, "This court's adjourned. Bar's open, boys!"

Whoops and cheers greeted the declaration, and the spectators surged toward the bar, carrying Herman Jeffords with them, slapping him on the back and congratulating him on his escape from Calvin's trap. The crowd had gotten a dramatic ending to this trial, even if it hadn't been the one they were expecting. Herman would have plenty of drinks bought for him before the night was over, and the whiskey might dull the pain of knowing that his own brother had tried to kill him.

Stark was ready for a beer himself, but as he turned toward the bar, he found Hamilton blocking his path. The prosecutor-politician was glaring at Stark with hate shining in his eyes. "I won't forget this," he said in a low voice just loud enough for Stark to hear over the uproar in the saloon. "You'll be sorry you showed me up this way in front of my constituents, Stark."

"What happened to all the flowery lawyer talk, Cassius?" Stark asked with a grin. "Hell, you don't sound like yourself no more."

"Just remember what I said." With that, Hamilton turned on his heel and stalked off through the crowd, obviously eager to leave the scene of his humiliation.

Jed Stockdale came up to Stark. "I meant what I said about paying you, mister—" he began, but once again Stark cut him off with a shake of the head.

"No need," Stark said.

Stockdale shrugged. "Well, suit yourself. Can I at least buy you a beer?"

"I reckon that'd be all right."

Stark and the old rancher each lifted a mug at the bar; then Stockdale thanked him again and left. He might have been cleared of murder, but he was still not well liked here in town. Stark got a refill and carried the mug of beer over to an empty table, where he sat down and watched the celebration around Herman Jeffords continuing.

Judge Buchanan walked over to the table holding a mug of his own, his gait only slightly unsteady. "Mind if I join you?" he asked.

Stark nodded toward one of the empty chairs. "Help yourself."

The judge settled down in the chair and sighed wearily. "We came too damned close to sending an innocent man to the hanging tree."

"It happens," Stark said.

"Well, we've you to thank that it didn't happen this time, Mr. Stark. Tell me . . . have you ever given any thought to becoming an attorney yourself?"

The question took Stark by surprise. He bought a little time by sipping the beer, then said, "I reckon the thought's crossed my mind a time or two. Never figured anybody'd take me seriously. Hell, I'm rough as a cob."

Buchanan leaned forward. "But any man who knows about the principle of habeas corpus is better educated in the law than half of the polecats calling themselves lawyers out here in the West.

Hell, some of them have never even *heard* of Blackstone, let alone studied him!"

Stark's wide shoulders rose and fell in a shrug. "I just never figured I had a chance—"

"Well, you do," Buchanan insisted. "What's a tort?"

"A civil wrong, not including a breach of contract, for which the injured party is entitled to compensation."

The judge grinned and took a healthy swallow of beer. As he wiped the back of his other hand across his mouth, he said, "When I asked that question of the last son of a bitch who said he wanted to be a lawyer, he told me it was either a fried pie or a whore, depending on who was doing the talking."

Stark gave a laugh while the judge took a swig of his beer.

"We know you know all about habeas corpus," Buchanan said as he lowered his mug to the table. "How about non compos mentis?"

"That's fancy talk for a fella who's plumb out of his head," replied Stark. "I figure that's something lawyers and judges would know plenty about."

The judge was taking another swallow of beer, and some of it must have gone down the wrong way, because he coughed and turned even redder in the face than normal and pounded a palm against the table. Gasping for breath, he said, "You're right about that. You got a copy of White and Wilson's *Practice and Pleading?*"

Stark nodded. "Read through it three times already."

"Don't overdo it," growled Buchanan. "Clients don't want their lawyer to be so damned educated that he's forgot everything he ever knew about being one of the common folks." The judge extended his hand to Stark and continued, "Your answers are good enough for me, son. I'm admitting you to the bar."

Stark glanced around at the saloon. "You mean I'm a lawyer now?"

"That's right. You can hang out your shingle, and I hope you'll practice here in Buffalo Flat. It'd be nice to have another lawyer around besides that windbag Hamilton."

"I'll give it some thought," Stark promised, hardly able to believe that his whole life had been changed just like that, with a simple question and a minimum of fuss. Suddenly he dug out his watch from the pocket of his jeans, flipped open the turnip, and checked the time. As he stowed the watch away again, he picked up his mug of beer with the other hand and drained it, then stood up. "But I'll have to see about setting up my practice later. Right now I got something else I have to do."

Judge Buchanan stared up at him. "What could be more important than starting your legal career?"

"I've got a run to finish," Big Earl said, "and you never can tell when some jasper'll get a foolish notion in his head to hold up that stage."

Chapter Two

Several months had passed since the trial of Jed Stockdale, and those months had shown Earl Stark just how quickly things can change. He had borrowed a branding iron and burned into a short length of plank the words he had thought he would never see: *Earl Stark, Attorney at Law.*

There was a vacant set of rooms for rent above Napier's Hardware Store, with a staircase leading up the outside of the building to the entrance. Stark used some of the money he had saved from his job with Martin Suggins's stage line to rent the rooms. One of them, the front room, would serve as his office, and he could easily live in the rest of the space. He didn't have many possessions and didn't need much room.

He bored holes in each end of the plank sign and hung it from the awning over the boardwalk at the bottom of the stairs. Judge Buchanan was on hand for the hanging of the "shingle," along with some of the other townspeople, and Stark was a little embarrassed by the fuss they made over him. But he felt mighty proud, nevertheless, and as he stepped back to gaze up at the sign, some instinct made him glance across the street.

Cassius P. Hamilton stood there on the other sidewalk wearing a fancy suit and top hat and tightly gripping a silver-headed walking stick in one hand. The politician glared at Stark, who was still dressed in his working clothes, then stalked off.

Stark looked down at himself. He was going to have to do something about his getup. A lawyer couldn't appear in court wearing a duster and jeans and an old cavalry shirt that had seen better days.

A few hours later Stark went over to Kelley's Mercantile and used more of his savings to buy a black suit, a gray vest, a few white shirts, and a string tie. He had his hat cleaned and freshly blocked at the haberdasher's. For a few minutes he thought about buying a pair of actual shoes to wear instead of his high-topped black boots, but he decided that would be going too far.

The quarters above the hardware store were already furnished, including a mirror in the bedroom, and when Stark put all the garb on and stood in front of the glass, he could scarcely believe his own eyes. He looked . . . well, almost distinguished. A broad grin crossed his face at the thought. You could dress up a hog, he told himself, but it was still a hog. Maybe this whole notion of practicing law was a mistake.

But as long as he was around Buffalo Flat, he would annoy the hell out of Cassius P. Hamilton, and there was something to be said for *that*.

He'd stick with it for a while and see what happened.

Less than a week later, he had his first case. A

couple of men who had run a freight line for several years were suing each other, each claiming the other had cheated him out of some of the firm's profits. One of the men retained Stark to represent him when the case came to trial before Judge Buchanan. Once again the bar at the Tumbling Dice was temporarily closed, since the town's courthouse was still under construction, but this time Stark went into the saloon to take a hand in the trial as an honest-to-God lawyer.

The case wasn't nearly as dramatic as the murder trial Stark had witnessed before, but when it was over, the parties had come to an amicable settlement—it seemed that both partners had never been very good at ciphering. The whole ruckus was over some bad arithmetic, rather than anybody really stealing anything—and Stark felt fairly satisfied as he joined Judge Buchanan afterward for a drink.

That was the first of quite a few cases to be adjudicated. Cassius P. Hamilton's private practice was limited to those who could afford to pay his steep fees, which meant that most of the businessmen and ranchers and farmers in the area couldn't hire him. Stark, on the other hand, felt a little uncomfortable charging anybody for his services, and more than once he was paid with a ham or a bushel of potatoes. Word got around that he was a reasonable man and a good lawyer, and he had all the work he could handle. There were wills to be drawn up, lawsuits to be tried, an occasional criminal case when he found himself defending a cowboy accused of disturbing the peace of rustling. Stark didn't win every case, but he worked hard at all of them, spending long hours and burning countless candles as he studied the law books he'd had freighted over from his rented room in the town of Whitehorse, where he'd lived before settling down in Buffalo Flat.

Judge Buchanan was a help, too. When the old jurist hadn't been tippling too much, he had a keen legal mind, and Stark considered all of the trials he took part in as learning experiences. In addition, another lesson began to soak in: Out here in the West, the spirit of the law was sometimes more important than the letter.

It was a letter that came in the mail, though, some six months after he had hung up his shingle, that had the biggest impact on Stark's life.

On that morning, with no clients in his office and no cases pending, Stark strolled down to the stage station to pass the time of day with Martin Suggins. The stage line owner looked up from the counter in the office as his burly former employee opened the door and stepped inside.

"Mornin', Martin," Stark said, then added, "I mean *good* morning." Lately he had been trying to talk more like a lawyer and less like the poorly educated stagecoach guard he had been not that long before.

"Hello, Earl," Suggins replied. "You haven't come to serve me with any papers, have you?"

Stark hooked his thumbs in the pockets of his

vest and leaned back slightly. "Now why in the world would I do that?"

"Seems that every time I see you, you're busy with some sort of law business."

"Nope. I just thought I'd come by and pass the time of day," Stark said.

Suggins smiled. "Well, I'm always glad to see you. Tell me, are you still feuding with Cassius Hamilton?"

"That fella sure doesn't like me," Stark admitted, "but he's gone back to Washington City. Left last week. Legislature's back in session again."

"Oh, yes, I remember now. I saw his name on one of the passenger lists. Took the stage to Whitehorse to catch the train there." Suggins glanced at the chalkboard just inside the door of the office. "Speaking of Whitehorse, the coach from there ought to be rolling in any minute."

True to his prediction, in only a few moments the sound of hoofbeats, the shouts of small boys, and the barking of dogs drifted in through the door Stark had left open. The arrival of a coach was always heralded by such a commotion. Stark turned toward the door as the coach rocked to a stop in the street outside. He could hear the creaking of the thoroughbraces as the vehicle settled and became still.

"Right on time," Suggins said proudly. "Must not have been any trouble on this leg of the run."

Stark ambled out onto the porch, Suggins following closely behind him. The driver, a crusty old gent named Lachman, spotted Stark and raised a hand in greeting. They had been paired on many a run over the past few years. Lachman had a new shotgun guard on the box beside him now, a wet-behind-the-ears kid named Mike Nolan. Stark had seen the youngster around Buffalo Flat but hadn't known that he had gone to work for the stage line.

"Howdy, Earl," called Lachman. "When're you goin' to get rid of that fancy suit and start ridin' these stages again, like you're 'sposed to?"

"Not anytime soon, I reckon," Stark replied with a grin.

"Any trouble?" Suggins asked as he looked up at the jehu.

"Not a bit," said Lachman. "Mike and me didn't see hide nor hair of any badmen." He reached down to the floorboard and lifted a thick leather pouch by its strap. "Here's the mail from Whitehorse."

Suggins took the mail pouch and motioned for the hostlers who had come out of the barn to get busy changing the teams. A couple of passengers got off the stage, but no one was waiting to board for the rest of the run over to Fisherton. While Suggins carried the mail inside, Stark stood beside the stagecoach to swap lies with Lachman, who remained perched on the box along with the guard. This stop wouldn't take long.

A few minutes later, while Stark was still talking with the driver, Suggins stepped onto the porch again and called, "Got a letter here for you, Earl."

Stark looked over in surprise. He had no relations that he knew of, and he hardly ever got letters. Only one person might be expected to write to him, really . . .

Stark felt his heart thudding a little harder and faster. "Be seein' you," he said to Lachman and went over to the porch to take the envelope Suggins held out toward him. His heartbeat sped up even more when he saw his name on the envelope and recognized the hand in which it was written.

His first impulse was to lift the envelope to his nose and smell it, figuring that he might still be able to catch a hint of Laura's perfume, but that would look silly out here in public, he decided. He turned it over a time or two in his blunt fingers and swallowed.

"Well," said Suggins, "aren't you going to open it?"

"Man's mail is his own business," growled Stark, feeling foolish. But Suggins didn't appear to be budging, and he could feel Lachman and young Nolan watching him as well. He worked a finger under the flap of the envelope at one end and tore it open.

Inside were several folded sheets of paper covered with a fine, precise handwriting. It was the same as the writing on the outside of the envelope, and Stark knew it well. He swallowed again, stuffed the sheets back in the envelope, and cleared his throat. "I'll read this later," he declared. "No hurry."

Suggins grinned. "Whatever you say, Earl. After all, a man's mail is his own business, or so I've been told."

"Damn right," Stark snapped. He turned, waved at Lachman and Nolan, and strode off down the street, well aware that the three men were watching him and probably chuckling.

Let 'em, he thought. A man needed privacy when he was reading a letter from a woman like Laura Delaney.

For once Stark was glad there were no potential clients waiting in his office when he got back to the rooms over the hardware store. He hung his hat on a set of antlers mounted on the wall just inside the door, then went behind the big desk in the corner of the front room where he conducted business. His large, sturdy, leather-covered chair creaked slightly as he lowered his weight onto it and opened the envelope again. Other papers were scattered around the top of the desk, but Stark had eyes only for the missive he held in his hands.

He turned to the last page first, eager to see her name. There it was, the pen strokes a little looser and more casually formed than the handwriting in the body of the letter: *Yrs. truly, Laura Delaney.*

Stark closed his eyes, and he could see her as plain as day. Hair the color of corn silk, eyes the color of the sky on a warm spring morning. A quick, mischievous smile, and a slender figure that moved with infinite grace. Lips as red as a

39

ripe strawberry and tasting just as sweet, the touch of warm and gentle fingertips . . . Stark remembered all those things, and he felt his insides tighten with longing as the memories washed over him.

It wasn't that anything, well, *improper* had ever gone on between them. He had courted Laura Delaney for six months or more, but he had always been a gentleman. Laura was a lady and wouldn't have stood for anything else. But she had allowed him to kiss her a few times, and they had both sensed the fire and passion lurking right underneath the surface, ready to break free if only they would give it a chance.

There was more to it than mere passion, though, Stark told himself. Laura was the smartest woman he had ever known, and she had her own opinions and wasn't afraid to express them. Most folks probably wouldn't have thought she was very well matched with a rough old bear like him, but the two of them had known better. The relationship would have gone a lot farther than some polite courting and a little sparking if only he had pressed his case. She would have married him.

Stark gave a little shake of his head. He'd had too much respect and affection for Laura to ask her to share the life of a man who risked death every time he left on a stagecoach. A woman like Laura deserved a husband whose job wasn't as dangerous as that of a shotgun guard.

Of course, he wasn't a shotgun guard anymore.

He was a lawyer now, a respected man in a stable profession. Maybe things would be different. He had thought before about writing to her, but he had been waiting until his practice was well established.

He turned back quickly to the first page of the letter and began reading in earnest, but before he reached the bottom of the page, he was straining to keep from crumpling the paper.

Stark's breath hissed between his teeth, and his pulse pounded inside his head. According to the words Laura had written, several of the young men in Whitehorse had begun paying suit to her now that Stark had moved to Buffalo Flat. That was to be expected, considering how attractive she was. But between the lines he read that she was considering accepting one of the many proposals of marriage that had come her way.

I know you will understand if I take whatever action may be necessary, Earl. . . .

The words on the paper blurred a little, and Stark reached into his vest pocket for the spectacles he sometimes wore for close work. He slipped the rimless spectacles over his eyes and concentrated on the letter, but the writing was still blurred.

His eyes were wet, he realized.

Stark put the letter down, took a deep breath, and spent a moment polishing his spectacles before settling them on his nose again. There,

41

that was better. The glass in the lenses must have been a little dirty after all, he told himself. He read on, but the chatty, friendly letter with its serious undertones was just more of the same. Laura had gotten her real message out of the way early.

Don't be surprised if I marry someone else, Earl, since you were too stupid and slow to ask me yourself.

She hadn't come right out and said it in so many words, but that was what she meant.

"Maybe it's not too late," Stark muttered aloud. He put her letter down, reached for a pen and inkwell, and searched through the clutter on the desk for a clean piece of paper. Maybe he still had a chance.

Dear Laura,

Perhaps this news has reached you already from some other source, but I have left the stage line and am now engaged in the practice of law here in Buffalo Flat. I would be very pleased and honored if you would consider visiting me here so that you can see how a ragged old buffalo such as myself can make something better of himself . . .

The pen scratched furiously on the paper as Stark continued writing, telling Laura about everything that had happened since a cracked

42

axle had gotten him involved with the murder trial of Jed Stockdale. His handwriting was legible but cramped, and he wished it was a little fancier. He wished he could come up with the flowery, romantic words he needed to tell her how he really felt about her. He had always been a plain-spoken man, though, and that carried over into his correspondence. Maybe he should just come right out and tell her he loved her and wanted to marry her. He considered the idea for a moment as he paused, pen poised over the page, then shook his head. Such a blunt declaration might frighten her off and cause her to refuse his invitation to come to Buffalo Flat for a visit. For a moment he thought about riding over to Whitehorse to see her, then discarded that approach as well. Folks here in Buffalo Flat admired him now, thinking of him as a lawyer and not as a stagecoach guard. He wanted Laura to see the new Earl Stark, Earl Stark the Respected Citizen. Then she could tell what she would be getting if she accepted the proposal he intended to make before she went back to Whitehorse.

She could still turn him down, of course, but Stark wasn't going to let himself even think about that possibility. He closed the letter with best wishes for her continued health, then leaned back in his chair and sighed, exhausted. This business of emotions was hard work. He'd rather face a whole passel of outlaws than have to write another letter like this.

The southbound stage to Whitehorse would be back through Buffalo Flat the next day, and Stark could get the letter in the mail pouch then. Once he'd posted it, there was only one thing he could do.

And that was wait.

Chapter Three

Three days later he received the reply he had been waiting for. Laura Delaney was not only glad to hear from him, but she was pleased to accept his invitation. He would have to arrange for a room for her at the local boardinghouse, of course, since everything would be open and aboveboard and respectable, but her letter also said that she hoped they could perhaps find the time to go for a ride in the country, or even a picnic.

Stark grinned when he read that. She was saying that she wanted him to court her again, and he was going to be glad to oblige.

Laura closed by saying that she would arrive on the stage from Whitehorse two days hence, and when that day dawned, Stark was up and about early, despite the fact that the coach wouldn't roll into Buffalo Flat until midafternoon.

He stopped in at Hukill's Tonsorial Parlor and had his beard and hair trimmed, then spent an extra four bits and had a bath in one of the big metal tubs in the bathhouse out behind the barbershop. Clean and smelling of bay rum, he went back to his rooms, dressed in fresh clothes, and settled down to wait. He spent the morning reading through the law books on the wall shelf behind his desk, then went down the street for lunch at the Red Top Café. The steak and potatoes he ordered were only half-eaten when he shoved the plate away, however; Stark was just too dadblasted nervous to be very hungry. He even turned down the dish of cherry cobbler the waitress offered him.

He left money on the table to pay for his meal, then went outside. Buffalo Flat was quiet today, not much traffic on the street, and those folks who were moving around didn't pay much attention to Stark. They didn't know this was the most important day of his life. The only one in town who might have an inkling of what was going on was Martin Suggins, who knew that Stark had sent a letter to Whitehorse and received another one from there as well.

Stark strolled up one side of the street and down the other, then paused in front of the livery stable and muttered a fervent "Hell!" It would be two more hours at least before the stagecoach arrived, maybe longer if there was any trouble along the way. Stark had waited months to see Laura again, but he wasn't sure now if he could wait two more hours.

There was nothing stopping him from riding out to meet the coach, he realized. He knew the road from Whitehorse as well as anybody and would have no trouble following it. If he rode out now, he could probably intercept it on the other side of the gap and ride on into town with it. If Lachman was the driver, and if the coach wasn't full, he would probably allow Stark to tie his horse on behind and ride inside with Laura.

The more Stark thought about it, the better he liked the idea. He glanced down at his dark suit and grimaced. He had wanted Laura's first glimpse of him to be in his lawyering getup instead of the trail clothes she was used to seeing him in, but how impressive would it be if he showed up in a suit so covered with dust you couldn't tell *what* color it was? Better to change clothes, he decided.

Since pausing in front of the livery stable was what had given him the idea, it took Stark only a second to step inside and ask Sandstrom, the owner of the place, to saddle up his Appaloosa. Sandstrom was agreeable, and while the liveryman was handling that, Stark hurried over to his rooms to change clothes.

When he emerged a few minutes later, he was wearing the duster, jeans, and cavalry shirt that had been his usual garb during his days as a shotgun guard. Out of habit he had strapped on his holster with the LeMat revolver, too, and picked up his Winchester as he left his rooms. He had never been a particularly good shot with a long gun, which was why his talents were more suited to the greener and the LeMat, but he took the Winchester anyway and slid it into the saddle boot when he picked up the horse from Sandstrom's place.

The animal was big and rangy, powerful

enough to carry Stark's weight and rather distinctive looking with its dappling of dark spots on its lighter hindquarters. In his previous job Stark had never had much need for a saddle horse, but he'd had the Appaloosa for several years and knew the horse was a dependable mount, not particularly fast but strong and able to run all day when it needed to. Now, he snugged the rifle into the boot, patted the horse on its shoulder, and swung up into the saddle.

He rode out of Buffalo Flat, his route taking him past the stage station. Martin Suggins was standing on the porch, and although he lifted a hand to wave, Stark rode on past without slowing. He was too anxious to see Laura again, so he settled for returning the wave and going on, ignoring the frown on the other man's face.

Quickly Stark put Buffalo Flat behind him, heading south along the trail toward Whitehorse. The country around here was mostly prairie, as the name of the community indicated, but several miles ahead of him in the distance, Stark could make out a low line of hills. The road passed through a gap in those hills and then proceeded on toward Whitehorse through terrain that was a little more rugged. Between Buffalo Flat and the gap, though, the trail was flat and straight, and Stark made good time, reaching the hills in less than an hour.

When the road sloped up, the Appaloosa took the incline without any break in the pace of its smooth trot. Stark turned his head at the crest and looked back over the plains to the north, able to see the buildings of Buffalo Flat in the far distance. His next glimpse of the town, he knew, would come with Laura at his side, and that thought made a grin spread across his bearded face.

A warm, southerly breeze was blowing, and Stark had covered another mile or so on horseback when the wind suddenly carried a series of faint popping noises to his ears. He reined in sharply and listened, hearing the sounds again. Now that he was stopped, he could distinguish a difference in some of the sounds. Intermingled with the sharper crackle of pistol fire were the heavy booms of a shotgun.

"Damn it!" grated Stark, and then he jammed the heels of his boots into the Appaloosa's flanks, sending the horse surging forward into a powerful gallop. Out here on the frontier, one or two shots might not mean anything, but that much gunfire could only signify trouble.

And somewhere up ahead there on the road, Stark thought, was the stagecoach carrying Laura!

He had never been the type of man to wear spurs and punish the animal he was riding, but at that moment he wished he had some sharp Mexican rowels to jab into the sides of the Appaloosa. He wanted all the speed he could possibly get out of the horse. He leaned forward in the saddle, one hand on the reins and one on his hat, as the wind of the Appaloosa's gallop caught the tails of his duster and whirled them behind him. He couldn't hear the gunshots anymore, and Stark didn't know if that was because they had stopped or because the rolling thunder of the horse's hoofbeats drowned out the continuing reports.

A ridge loomed up in front of them, and the Appaloosa took it smoothly. At the top of the slope the road turned sharply and started down the hill on the far side. From that vantage point, Stark could see all the way across a wide, semiarid valley where a broad river might have run in some long distant, prehistoric past. About halfway across the valley, a plume of dust rose into the sky, kicked up by the hooves of a six-horse hitch and the iron-rimmed wheels of the Concord coach they were pulling. Twenty yards behind the coach rode a handful of men, firing after the fleeing vehicle.

Stark jerked the Appaloosa to a halt again and reached for the Winchester. The stagecoach was at least half a mile away, and the men chasing it could reach it a lot faster than Stark could from up here on the ridge. But maybe he could slow them down a mite, he thought as he lifted the rifle and levered a shell into the chamber. The Winchester bucked against his shoulder as he squeezed the trigger.

The range was too far for accurate shooting, but all he wanted to do was throw a scare into the outlaws chasing the stage. He had seen enough holdups, fought off enough would-be desperadoes, to be certain of what he was witnessing now. Those horsebackers were out to stop the stage and loot it of whatever valuables it might be carrying.

Stark fired four more times, using up a third of the fifteen cartridges carried in the Winchester's tubular magazine. The Appaloosa stood steady underneath him, accustomed to the sound of gunfire. Stark lowered the rifle and peered through the dust haze in the air. None of the bandits had pitched from their saddles; he hadn't really expected that. But they weren't pulling back, either. Obviously his shots hadn't come close enough to spook them.

Muttering curses, Stark was about to heel the horse into motion again when the stagecoach reached a sharp curve in the road around a grove of stubby trees. He saw the coach start to tilt, and the sight jolted an exclamation out of him. "Damn it, no! You're going too fast!"

The driver—at this distance Stark couldn't tell who he was—tried valiantly to bring the careening vehicle back under control, but the coach had already tipped too far to the side. With a crash that even Stark could hear, the stagecoach went over on its side, tumbling crazily and taking the team with it in a welter of trailing and tangled lines, flailing hooves, and shrill whinnies of pain and fright.

Stark felt his insides wrench in fear, not for himself but for the driver, the guard, and the passengers in the coach. He kicked the Appaloosa into a run down the hill as his eyes searched the scene of the crash for any sign of life. The outlaws were much closer and were going to get there first, no question of that, but Stark wanted to lend a hand to any survivors who might be inside.

Including Laura.

His heart lurched at that thought, but he shoved his worry for her to the back of his mind. For the time being, he had to concentrate on the immediate problem, which was dealing with the outlaws. The big Appaloosa covered the distance as quickly as could be expected, but Stark saw with dismay that he was just too damned far away.

Two figures appeared on the ground near the coach, one of them scrambling to his feet, the other getting up more shakily. That would be the driver and the guard, Stark realized. They must have leapt clear when the coach went over; otherwise they would have been crushed when it rolled. As the outlaws swept up on horseback, the two men jerked out their pistols and started blasting. They were in the open, though, too far away from the coach to use it for cover, and the deadly outcome of this unfair duel was inevitable.

A volley of fire ripped out from the riders, and the driver and the guard were thrown backward, riddled with outlaw lead. Stark cursed bitterly again and opened up with the Winchester, but the back of a galloping horse was no place for accurate shooting.

The outlaws heard the shots and hurried their actions, one man swinging down from his horse to grab the mail pouch while two more dragged the strong-box clear of the coach, which had come to rest lying on its side. A couple of shots blasted open the lock on the express box, and the men scooped out its contents. Stark saw them hurrying back to their horses with their arms full of what looked like canvas bags.

The Winchester ran dry, and Stark jammed it back in its sheath. He didn't bother reaching for the LeMat. At any range over thirty feet, the Frenchman's invention wasn't worth firing.

The bandits leapt back on their horses, wheeled the animals around, and galloped off, heading west away from the trail. Stark thought about angling after them to intercept them, but then he looked again at the overturned coach. There was more movement around it now as folks began to crawl out of the wreckage.

He had to check on Laura, make sure she was all right. Chasing after the robbers was going to have to wait.

As he neared the coach, Stark searched frantically for a flash of Laura's blond hair in the sunlight or the sight of her familiar slender figure, but he saw no sign of her. A cold ball of fear was forming in his belly as he reined in and practically threw himself from the saddle. Three men and one woman were dusting themselves off. One of the men was holding his arm in such a peculiar position that Stark knew the bone had to be broken, and another had a long, bloody gash on his forehead. The woman was weeping and wailing almost uncontrollably. She wasn't injured as far as Stark could see, but she had to have been frightened out of her wits by the holdup and the crash.

Maybe Laura hadn't even been on the stage, Stark told himself. Maybe she had missed it for some reason.

He grabbed the arm of one of the male passengers and asked, "Is there anybody else inside?"

The man just stared at him groggily, his dazed state probably the result of a hard knock on the head when the coach overturned. Stark turned toward the other men, the one with the broken arm and the one with the bloody face, and was about to ask them the same question when the crying woman suddenly grabbed his arm.

"She's inside!" the woman said hysterically. "Oh my God, you've got to help her!"

Stark caught her shoulders and, restraining the urge to shake her, demanded, "There was another woman in the coach?" "A young woman, a pretty young woman . . . Oh, Lord, I thought we were all going to die!"

Stark took a step toward the coach and shoved the babbling woman aside when she continued to clutch at him. Using a wheel and one of the thoroughbraces for support, he clambered up onto the side of the overturned vehicle and looked down through the open door. There he could see a huddled shape lying against the side of the coach resting on the ground.

Stark's senses were numb with disbelief as he

lowered himself carefully through the door into the coach. His boots landed on the opposite door, and he crouched beside the woman lying there. She wore a hat, and her jacket had gotten pulled up over her face during the crash, obscuring her features. Gently Stark lowered the folds of cloth, revealing the lovely face that had been so vivid in his memory. Laura was pale now, too damned pale, but there was a whisper of breath coming from her open mouth.

She was alive.

Stark knelt there, unsure what to do next. He was no doctor, but he could tell something was badly wrong. Laura's head was twisted at an angle that couldn't be natural. He eased her hat off and let the thick blond hair spill over his fingers, then carefully slid his hand under her head to support it. As he did, her blue eyes opened and stared up at him in a mixture of shock and pain and recognition.

"Earl?" she whispered.

"That's right, Laura," he said, making his voice sound as strong and confident as he could. "I'm here now, and those outlaws are long gone. You're going to be all right, honey."

"I . . . I can't feel anything, Earl."

Her voice was weak, and Stark had trouble making out the words. But she repeated them, panic edging into her voice and making it stronger.

Stark felt the coldness inside him intensify. He reached down with his other hand and caught her fingers, which lay loosely at the end of an equally limp arm. Squeezing tightly, he asked, "Can you feel that?"

"Feel . . . what? I can't . . . feel anything."

Stark's tongue felt thick in his mouth as he tried to lick lips gone as dry as the desert. He had never been one to lie, but now was a good time to start. How could he tell her that her neck was broken?

"It . . . it's bad . . . isn't it?"

"Bad enough," Stark said with a nod. He had watched men die before, and sometimes they had been good friends. But he had never watched life fade from the eyes—the beautiful blue eyes—of a woman he loved and wanted to make his wife.

"I was . . . so looking forward . . . to seeing you again . . . Earl," Laura said, struggling to get the words out.

Stark leaned over her. "Shhh. You just lay quiet now. Somebody'll be along to help us."

That was a lie, too. No one was coming, and even if they were, it would be too late.

Laura looked up at him and said, "I won't . . . be quiet . . . Too much to say . . . I have to . . . say it now."

Stark felt as if somebody had made a hole in him and scooped out his insides, leaving him hollow. He managed to say, "I'm listening, Laura."

"I . . . I know why . . . you wrote to me. I was hoping you would . . . understand. I didn't want to . . . marry any of those boys . . . back in Whitehorse. I wanted . . . you, Earl."

"I was going to ask you to marry me when you came to Buffalo Flat," he told her, his own voice sounding to him like it was coming from a million miles away.

"I know. And my answer . . . would have been . . . yes. I love you, Earl."

There was a peculiar gusting sound to her voice as she whispered his name, and even as he said, "I love you, too, Laura," he knew it was too late. Nothing was left there now, no spark of life in her eyes, no warmth in her. Gone, all gone.

Still holding her gently, Stark lifted her body, clutched her to his broad chest, and wept. For a moment, a few brief seconds that seemed like an eternity to him, his powerful frame shook with grief and rage. Then, as carefully as ever, he lowered her to the side of the coach once more. No matter how badly he was hurting, he still had things to do.

Leaving Laura's body in the coach, he climbed out and went quickly to the sprawled figures of the driver and the guard. As he had feared, he saw the faces of Lachman and young Mike Nolan contorted in death. Shaken from the crash, outnumbered and on foot, they'd never had a chance against the mounted killers.

The passenger who had been knocked addlepated by the wreck was starting to get his wits back now. Stark told the woman to look after the gent with the broken arm, and having that responsibility seemed to calm her down some. Stark went over to the other man and asked, "How bad are you hurt?"

Gingerly the man touched the gash on his forehead. "I reckon I'll have one hell of a headache and a mighty ugly scar, but I'm all right."

"Good," grunted Stark. "You and me and that other hombre have got to get that coach upright again. Otherwise it'll be a long walk into Buffalo Flat."

One of the horses in the team was already dead, and two others were so badly hurt that Stark had to put them out of their misery with the LeMat. He cut the others loose from their harnesses and got them on their feet again, one at a time, tying the dangling lines to a nearby mesquite so they wouldn't wander off. All of the surviving animals were pretty spooked. Stark thought they could be hitched up again and would be able to pull the coach, though.

He and the two relatively healthy male passengers tried to lift the coach back onto its wheels, but it was too heavy. Stark got his rope from the Appaloosa's saddle and tied one end to the railing around the top of the coach, then fashioned the other into a double-rigged harness, which he attached to two of the remaining horses. The woman used her hat with its tall feather to swat the rumps of the animals and start them pulling while Stark and the two men heaved against the coach. Slowly, it began to tip back to an upright position, then finally crashed down on all four wheels. Stark didn't allow himself to think about how Laura's body was being tumbled around inside.

The wheels and the axles weren't cracked or broken, and Stark knew the coach would make Buffalo Flat without much trouble. That was lucky. So was the fact that three of the teamers had survived the crash. He got them hitched up again, along with the Appaloosa, though the horse gave Stark a look as if it resented being used to pull a mere stagecoach.

Before Stark would allow the passengers to climb aboard again, he rummaged through the boot at the back of the vehicle and found a large square of canvas big enough to wrap Laura's body in. He tucked the canvas carefully around her, smoothing the hair away from her face before he covered it up. He used another square of canvas to cover the bullet-riddled bodies of Lachman and Mike Nolan after placing them inside the vehicle. Then the other woman and the man with the broken arm climbed inside the coach. The remaining two men elected to ride up top, one on the roof and one on the box beside Stark, who took up the reins he had pieced back together.

"Have you ever handled a coach before?" the man asked, holding a bandanna to the gash on his forehead.

"A time or two," snorted Stark. "Besides, I've watched the best in the business. Don't worry, mister, I'll get this coach to Buffalo Flat."

"I wish you'd showed up a little sooner,

friend," the man mused as Stark got the make-shift team moving and the coach lurched forward.

Stark nodded grimly. That thought had already occurred to him. If he had been the guard on this run, Laura Delaney might still be alive, and there would likely be some dead outlaws roasting in hell this very minute.

But the outlaws' date with the devil had only been postponed, Stark vowed to himself as the stage rolled toward Buffalo Flat. He intended to hunt down every one of those killers and see to it that they met justice—either at the end of a rope or the barrel of a gun.

Chapter Four

By the time the stagecoach reached Buffalo Flat, the grief Stark was feeling had receded into a dull ache throbbing deep inside him, filling up the emptiness he had experienced earlier. A part of his brain flirted with disbelief as well. It was ridiculous, just ridiculous. Laura couldn't be dead. Why, he had been planning to ask her to marry him, and he was sure she would have said yes. They were going to get married and raise a bunch of kids and be happy. That wouldn't happen if she was dead. So it just couldn't be true.

But it was, and most of Stark's mind knew it. He handled the reins and kept the team moving out of habit and instinct, because his conscious thoughts were full of the lovely, golden-haired young woman who had been taken away from him so cruelly.

The stage was late. With only four horses— one of them Stark's Appaloosa—instead of the usual six pulling, the townspeople were alerted right away that something was very wrong. Folks trotted alongside the coach as Stark piloted it down the street, but he ignored the questions they shouted up at him. He kept his eyes fixed on the stage station up ahead, knowing that he had to concentrate on this goal in order to reach it.

Martin Suggins hurried outside in response to the growing commotion, worry etched into his thin face. His eyes widened at the sight of Stark handling the reins, and the bloody-faced man sitting beside the burly lawyer was further proof that something terrible had occurred.

"My God, Earl!" Suggins cried as Stark brought the coach to a stop in front of the station. "What happened?"

"Holdup," Stark grunted as he dropped the reins and sat there on the box, his shoulders slumped. "Down on the other side of the gap. Lachman and Nolan were both killed."

"One of the women in the coach was killed, too," added the man sitting beside Stark.

Stark flinched a little, as if he had been struck. He hadn't told the passengers about his relationship with Laura, but they must have known how deeply her death had affected him from the way he looked and acted. The man beside him muttered, "Sorry," then began climbing down from the box.

No point in sitting there, Stark told himself. He stepped down from the coach, too, and turned to face Suggins. The stage line owner was pale and distraught as he said to one of the bystanders, "Fetch Sheriff Bishop." Then he put a hand on Stark's arm and asked, "Are you all right, Earl?"

"I'm fine," Stark replied curtly. "I threw some lead at the bandits who chased the stage, but I was too far away to do any good. Then the coach turned over when Lachman tried to take a curve too fast. The outlaws killed Lachman and Nolan and grabbed the mail pouch and looted the strongbox before I could get there."

"Did they rob the passengers?"

Stark shook his head. "They took off as soon as they had the pouch and what was in the box, so I reckon I spooked 'em at least a little. They headed west, toward the Maricopa hills."

"Lord, this is awful. And there was a woman killed, too?"

"Her name was Laura Delaney."

Stark's flat declaration made Suggins look sharply at him. "I remember that name," the stage line owner said. "That was the woman who wrote to you from Whitehorse. You sent a letter back to her—"

"She was coming here to visit me. That's how come I rode out to meet the stage." That was all Stark said.

At that moment, Sheriff Pete Bishop and his deputies came running up in response to the summons of the townie who had gone to the sheriff's office. Bishop was a tall, blond-haired man, older than his youthful appearance indicated, who had been a lawman for quite some time. He had plenty of questions for Stark while his deputies took the injured folks over to the office of the local doctor for treatment. Stark went through the whole story again, just as he had begun telling it to Suggins; it wasn't any less páinful the second time around.

Bishop listened intently, then turned to Suggins and asked, "You got any idea what was in that express box, Martin?"

"A shipment of money for the bank," the stage line owner replied, bitterness in his voice.

The sheriff raised an eyebrow in surprise, and Stark stared at Suggins, too. "How come I didn't know anything about this money coming in?" Bishop asked.

"Harvey Dumas over at the bank wanted me to keep it quiet," Suggins said as he rubbed his temples. "He said the fewer people who knew about it, the better, and since he's the president of the bank, I went along with him. Damn! I knew I should have put on some extra guards or something, but at the same time I didn't want to do anything out of the ordinary." He looked over at Stark and added peevishly, "This might not have happened if you hadn't quit me, Earl."

Stark's temper threatened to explode at that accusation, but with an effort he reined in his anger. Besides, the same thought had already crossed his mind, and he couldn't blame Suggins for having it occur to him, too. "If I'd been riding shotgun, it damn sure *wouldn't* have happened."

Suggins shook his head regretfully. "I'm sorry, Earl. I . . . I didn't really mean it like that. Things haven't been going very well. Half a dozen coaches have been held up lately. I've had passengers robbed and terrorized and express boxes

64

stolen. Word's gotten around that Big Earl isn't riding the coaches anymore, and that's made the outlaws a lot braver than they used to be."

Stark frowned darkly. He didn't want to think about the implications of what Suggins had just said, but he had no choice. "You mean my quitting and becoming a lawyer has led to your coaches being robbed?"

"Like Martin said, word's gotten around," Bishop put in before Suggins could answer. "But you can't blame yourself, Earl. A man's got a right to better himself, and that's all you did by becoming a lawyer."

Stark turned away from the other men, his hands gripping the railing that ran along the front of the porch so tightly that it felt as if he could rip the top rail right off. A huge shudder went through him. He'd had no idea things had gotten so bad in the area. He had been so busy with his law practice that he'd ignored everything else. If he had realized that the stages had recently been hit more often—and for sure if he had known there was a shipment of money coming in on the same coach as Laura—he never would have allowed her to take the stage. He would have rented a buggy and gone to Whitehorse to get her himself. And he would have protected her every damned foot of the way.

But now it was too late. She was dead and gone, and it was his fault.

His head had been hanging, but now it lifted sharply, jolted up by anger and sorrow and guilt.

65

It wasn't entirely his fault, he thought. Maybe he had contributed indirectly to the situation, but the men who were directly to blame for Laura's death were the low-down buzzards who had robbed that stage.

They were the ones who would pay.

The undertaker, a fussy little man named Floyd who sported a thin mustache and pomaded hair, came bustling up to Bishop. "I'm told my services are required here, Sheriff."

The lawman gestured toward the coach. "There are three bodies inside, one lady and a couple of good hombres. Treat 'em right, Floyd."

"Always, Sheriff, always," assured the undertaker. He and the two assistants who had followed him up the street got busy, and Stark turned away, unwilling to watch.

Bishop rested a hand on his shoulder. "Come on, Earl. Let's go down to the Dice and have a drink. I reckon you could use one about now."

Stark started to pull away, then relented. A drink wouldn't make him feel any better, he thought, but Bishop was a good man and was trying to help. The least Stark could do was allow him that much. Besides, that would give him an opportunity to discuss the outlaws with Bishop. The lawman might have some idea where to start looking for them.

As Stark and Bishop started down the boardwalk, Bishop looked over his shoulder and said, "I'll be back to talk to you more about that money shipment, Martin. I'll want to have words with you and Harvey Dumas both."

Suggins nodded, evidently still too stunned by what had happened to look dismayed over the prospect of a rawhiding from Bishop about keeping important secrets from the law.

No one stopped Stark and Bishop on their way to the saloon to offer their condolences. The people of Buffalo Flat were unaware of his connection with the dead woman inside the stagecoach. For this Stark was vaguely grateful. Maybe later the good memories of his too-short time with Laura would resurface and become stronger, but right now all he had left was his pain, and he didn't want to share it with anybody. He was going to embrace it, draw strength from it, let it nurture the hatred he felt growing inside him. That was the only way he was going to be able to stand it.

Bishop led him to a table in the back corner of the barroom and signaled the bartender to bring them a couple of drinks. When the man came over to the table, Bishop said curtly, "Leave the bottle."

The bartender frowned. "You sure, Sheriff? That ain't like—"

"I said leave the bottle," snapped Bishop as he rattled a coin on the table. The bartender shrugged and placed the whiskey and a pair of shot glasses between the two men, then scooped up the money and went back behind the hardwood.

Bishop tipped amber liquid into the glasses and shoved one over to Stark. "There you go, Earl. Try some of that who-hit-John."

Stark picked up the whiskey, tossed it off without even tasting it or feeling any effect from the fiery stuff. Setting down the glass, he said, "Getting me drunk's not going to help anything, Pete."

"You're taking this holdup mighty personal, Earl—"

Bishop broke off at the look on Stark's face, realizing more was going on here than what he knew.

Quietly, Stark said, "That woman who was killed when the stage turned over . . . I was going to marry her."

Stunned, Bishop murmured, "Lord, I'm sorry, Earl. I didn't have any idea—"

"I know you didn't. Nobody around here does, except maybe Martin Suggins." Stark shook his head. "No use in talking about that now. Tell me about the stage holdups around here."

Bishop shrugged. "Well, like Suggins said, he's had about half a dozen coaches hit in the past couple of months. All the robberies happened between here and Whitehorse, and the bandits have vanished over in the Maricopas each time. My deputies and I have tried to track them, but they're a slick bunch, Earl. They've given us the slip each time."

"What's over there in the Maricopas?"

"Not much," Bishop said. "There're some

settlements on the other side of the hills, but that's pretty rugged, isolated country between here and there. And out of my jurisdiction, too, when you come right down to it, but I never minded chasing those thieves up into the hills, since the robberies took place here in the county. I just wish I could've caught up with them before now."

Stark couldn't manage to muster up any anger toward the sheriff for failing to catch the outlaws before they could pull this latest robbery. Bishop was a good lawman and had undoubtedly done his best. Stark asked, "You think it's the same gang each time?"

"Looks like it to me. Can't say for sure, though, unless we apprehend some of them."

Stark leaned back in his chair and pushed his glass forward for Bishop to refill it. Talking about the situation had calmed him a little, gotten his mind to working in addition to his emotions. "I can't believe I haven't heard anything about this before now."

"Well, you been pretty busy, and Suggins hasn't exactly been spreading the news around. You can't blame him; a bunch of robberies will really play hob with the stage line's business. He's lost several valuable shipments, too, and he's on shaky ground financially, even with the insurance company making up most of the losses."

Stark nodded, understanding better now why Suggins had been angry with him for a moment. The man's business was in trouble, and he traced that back to Stark's leaving the job as shotgun guard, even though the connection was a tenuous one.

"You taking a posse out?" Stark asked after a moment.

Bishop nodded. "I reckon the boys are rounding up some volunteers right now. You looked so shook up I wanted to talk to you first, though. You riding with us?"

"Damn right," snapped Stark. "Think you can trail those sons of bitches? I can show you right where the holdup took place."

"That's what I'm counting on," Bishop replied. "Maybe this time we'll catch up to them. But Earl . . . if we do, I'll have to bring them in to stand trial legal-like, if they'll let me. I won't be a party to any vigilante justice."

Stark nodded, not expecting anything different from a man like Pete Bishop, although as far as Stark was concerned the outlaws had already been tried and convicted.

He was a lawyer, he reminded himself. He shouldn't be thinking things like that. The West wasn't quite the lawless wilderness it had once been, and now there was a right way to do things and a wrong way.

"Don't worry, Pete," he said. "I won't give you any trouble. Let's ride."

Bishop nodded, and the two men stood up and left the saloon, ready to join the posse that was forming on the main street of Buffalo Flat.

The biggest enemy of the pursuers was time. The sun was sliding down toward the hills where the stagecoach bandits had vanished, and once darkness fell, it would be impossible to follow the tracks the outlaws had left on the dusty ground.

For the moment, though, the trail leading away from the spot on the road where the holdup had occurred was plain enough to see, and the posse led by Sheriff Pete Bishop rode hard toward the west, following the hoofprints left by the horses of the gang.

Stark rode alongside Bishop, his bearded face set in grim lines. The sight of the dead horses from the stagecoach team reinforced memories that had not yet begun to fade. He tried to shove the thoughts of Laura's death out of his mind and concentrate instead on the trail he and the other members of the posse were following.

Bishop had brought along only two of his deputies, leaving the others behind in Buffalo Flat in case of trouble, but there were over a dozen citizens riding with the lawmen. A few of them were storekeepers, but most of the possemen were cowboys who had been in town when news of the robbery spread. They were well armed, knew how to use the guns they carried, and would give a good account of themselves in any fight. Stark knew that if the posse caught up to them, the bandits wouldn't stand much of a chance; they would have no choice but to surrender or be blown out of their saddles.

The posse reached the Maricopa hills late in the afternoon. The heights were steep, rugged, and rocky, although not very tall. With Bishop in the lead, the men from Buffalo Flat followed the outlaws' tracks along a sandy-bottomed canyon that wound through the hills. The layer of sand on the bottom of the canyon grew thinner before the trail reached the other side of the Maricopas, however, and eventually the sand ran out altogether, leaving only bare rock. Along with the sand, the tracks the posse had been following disappeared as well.

"They're smart, damn their sorry hides," Bishop sighed as he reined his horse to a halt and glared down at the stone floor of the canyon. "I don't even see any horseshoe scratches on that rock. They must've wrapped their horses' hooves."

Stark bit back a curse as he studied the canyon floor and came to the same conclusion. The outlaws had employed an old but effective trick to avoid leaving tracks. A horseshoe would sometimes make small marks even on rock; such a trail was difficult to follow but not impossible. But with the hooves wrapped in rawhide or burlap, even that sign was eliminated.

"Getting dark, anyway," Bishop went on. "Chances are we wouldn't have been able to follow them."

"So you're giving up?" snapped Stark, his tone accusatory. "Turning back?"

"I don't see as we've got much choice, Earl."

Bishop was holding his own temper with an obvious effort. "Those outlaws could be forted up somewhere ahead of us, and I'm not going to lead these men into an ambush. We'd be trailing blind, anyway. They've given us the slip, just like before."

"You, maybe," grunted Stark. "Not me." He nudged the Appaloosa forward.

Riding into the gathering darkness in the canyon, though, he could feel the weariness of the animal under him. The Appaloosa had been run hard today, without a chance for rest. It was one thing to push himself to the limit, Stark realized, but quite another to ask for such an effort from his horse.

Stubbornly he pushed ahead, walking the horse around a bend of the canyon and not looking back at the posse he'd soon left behind. The sun was down, leaving a rosy glow in the western sky, but here in this steep-sided slash in the hills, very little light penetrated. Stark could see well enough to know where he was going, but there was no way he could make out any tracks, even if some had been there for him to see. Maybe later, when the stars came out and the moon rose.

He glanced up at the sky, and his eyes narrowed. He saw something there, a thin black line against the gray of the onrushing night. Whatever it was, Stark lost sight of it. He reined in sharply and studied the sky, but he couldn't find the thing he had seen.

It had looked for all the world like a tendril

of smoke, he thought, and it was little short of miraculous that he had even seen it under the circumstances. Somebody up in the hills had a fire going. The outlaws? That was possible, all right, but it was equally likely the smoke—if that was what it was—had come from the fire of a prospector or a hardscrabble farmer trying to coax a living out of these thinly soiled hillsides. From everything Stark had heard, the Maricopas didn't have many people in them, but the hills weren't completely deserted, either.

A shiver ran through him. Somebody could be watching him right now, maybe even peering at him over the barrel of a rifle.

He lifted a hand and rubbed his tired eyes. Bishop had been right; the logical part of Stark's mind knew that. The trail was gone, and only a fool would chase after outlaws in the dark.

But the murderous bunch had to have gone somewhere. Either they were still here in the hills or they had headed for one of those distant settlements Bishop had mentioned. Whichever it was, somewhere along the way they would leave another trail, a trail Stark could find once the sun was up again.

With a sigh that held all the sorrow and anger and disappointment roiling around inside him, Stark turned the Appaloosa around and headed out of the hills.

He caught up with the posse before it reached Buffalo Flat, and Bishop was glad to see him. As

74

they rode into town, the sheriff said, "I can't very well go poking around over there on the other side of the Maricopas, Earl. Like I told you, that territory's out of my jurisdiction. But there's nothing stopping a private citizen like you from having a look-see around that part of the country, and if you find out anything, just let me know and I'll come arunnin' with a posse."

"Thanks, Pete. You knew I'd be riding that way again, didn't you?"

Bishop grinned faintly in the darkness. "I figured it'd be a pretty safe bet."

Stark bid the lawman good-night as the posse broke up, then left the Appaloosa at the livery stable with orders for Sandstrom to rub him down and give him plenty of grain. He walked from the stable to the hardware store and wearily climbed the stairs on the outside of the building.

He wouldn't have thought that one flight of stairs could be such a long walk, but he was dreading the rest of the night. As long as he was moving around, trying to accomplish something, he had been able to cope, to keep functioning. Now he faced long hours of nothing but memories and regrets. Maybe he should have stopped by the Tumbling Dice and reclaimed that bottle Bishop had bought. Getting good and drunk might be the only thing that would get him through the night.

The law office was dark when Stark stepped into it. Familiar with its furnishings, he had no trouble moving across the room in the dark and

75

finding the lamp on the desk. He broke off a lucifer from the clump of them in the pocket of his duster, then scratched the soft sulphur match to life and held the flame to the wick of the lamp. When it caught, he lowered the lamp's chimney and looked around as soft yellow light filled the room.

Everything about it rubbed him the wrong way—the desk, the big leather chair, the antlers on the wall that served as a hat rack. And especially the law books on their shelf above the desk, sitting there and seeming to mock him. He had submerged himself in those books and in his own life for months, never realizing the important things going on around him.

Never realizing that the time he might have had with Laura was running out.

Without thinking about what he was doing, Stark reached up and swept the law books off the shelf, sending them crashing to the floor in the corner. He trembled with the urge to stomp them with his booted feet or rip out their pages. Destroying the books wouldn't bring Laura back, though, Stark told himself. He could pull the whole office down around his ears and it wouldn't do a damned bit of good. She would still be dead.

He threw his hat and duster aside, not paying any attention to where they landed. Those law books would make a dandy little bonfire, he thought, then discarded the idea just as fast. He was on the verge of losing control, and he knew it.

Stark took a deep breath and placed his hands on top of the desk, palms down. He pressed hard with them, letting one shudder after another go through him. He clung to the thought of vengeance, but he had something more important than simple revenge to consider here.

Justice. And if it was going to come to those men who so richly deserved it, Stark was going to have to keep a clear head. A grim smile plucked at his lips as he whispered the word that was going to be his anchor from now on.

"Justice . . ."

"Good Lord, man, I've seen dogs drag in things that look better than you!"

Stark grinned ruefully at Judge Tobias Buchanan's exclamation. The judge was sitting at a corner table in the Red Top, having his breakfast. Buchanan lowered the steaming cup of coffee he held in his hand as Stark pulled out a chair and sat opposite him.

"It was a rough night," Stark said simply.

"You look like you slept in those clothes."

"Didn't seem any point in doing otherwise when I knew I'd be riding out again early this morning."

Buchanan pushed aside what was left of his bacon, fried eggs, and flapjacks. "I heard about what happened," he said solemnly. "Pete Bishop told me all about it when the posse got back last night. I'm sorry, Earl. Truly sorry."

"Thanks," Stark muttered. "But that doesn't

change anything. I just came by here because I figured you'd be having breakfast about now. Wanted to say so long before I rode out."

Looking askance at the saddlebags slung over Stark's shoulder and the greener in his left hand, the judge asked, "What do you mean? You're not leaving town, are you?"

Stark tossed a key onto the table in front of Buchanan. "That's the key to my place. I'd appreciate it if you'd look after it while I'm gone, Judge."

Buchanan frowned disapprovingly at him and said, "You're going after those outlaws, aren't you?"

"I don't know anything else to do."

"You could let the law handle it. Hell, you're an officer of the court. You can't go haring off after a bunch of desperadoes like some . . . some bounty hunter!"

"If you talked to Bishop, you must know that the trail petered out in the Maricopas," Stark said as he caught the eye of the waitress and pointed to Buchanan's coffee cup, signaling for her to bring him some of the strong black brew, too. He went on, "His authority runs out on this side of the hills. If anybody's going to keep looking for those outlaws, it's got to be me."

"Or the authorities in the next county."

Stark shook his head. "I looked at a map of the territory last night after I got back to town and calmed down a little. The county seat's way the hell up in the north end of the county at

78

Garrison City. The sheriff over there isn't going to be interested in poking around the Maricopas or those settlements on the other side of them."

"You don't know that," Buchanan declared. "It looks to me like you're just finding an excuse for taking the law in your own hands, Earl."

Stark was tired of arguing. He took a healthy swallow of the coffee the waitress placed in front of him, burning his mouth but feeling the bracing effect of the hot liquid. Nothing like some Arbuckle's to clear a man's head and get him moving in the morning, as countless cowboys had found out in trail camps over the years. Stark had been on a few drives in his younger days, and he remembered it well.

"I'm sorry, Judge," he said. "All I know is that I can't sit around here and go on like nothing's happened when those killers are riding free somewhere."

"So you're prepared to throw away your legal career to go after them?"

"I'll be back one of these days, don't worry." Stark swallowed more coffee and then stood up. He hadn't had any breakfast, but he wasn't hungry. "My horse ought to be saddled and ready to go by now."

Buchanan glowered at him. "You'll be back if you don't get yourself killed first. That's what you really mean."

From somewhere Stark found another grin as he hefted the greener and adjusted the saddlebags on his shoulder. "Don't worry, Judge. I may not be riding shotgun anymore, but I'm still Big Earl."

With that, he turned and walked out of the café.

Judge Buchanan watched him go, then slowly shook his head and said half to himself, "I hope that's enough, my friend. I hope that's enough."

Chapter Five

The Appaloosa was well rested this morning, and Stark could tell quite a difference in the horse as he rode toward the Maricopas, following the trail from the site of the robbery. As he moved into the hills, he thought about Laura. Her body would be taken back to Whitehorse in the undertaker's wagon today, so that her funeral could be held in the community where her family still lived. Stark would miss the funeral, and he felt a twinge of regret and guilt at the thought.

Folks had to mourn in their own way, though, and his way was to track down the skunks responsible for Laura's death and bring them to justice.

He rode through the same canyon he and Bishop and the others had followed the trail into the night before. This time, Stark pushed on, riding several miles past the point where the bottom of the canyon turned into solid rock and the tracks disappeared. He watched for side canyons but did not pass any, and his hope began to grow. If this pass was the only easy way through the hills, then it was more likely the outlaws had followed it all the way to the other side of the Maricopas. And once they emerged from the hills, they should have left tracks again, tracks that Stark could follow.

Keeping his eye on the sky, just in case he might spot smoke rising in the same place as on the evening before, Stark followed the canyon through the hills and finally emerged on the far side of the Maricopas. He reined in and studied the ground where some sparse cheat grass grew in the thin soil. Up ahead, the terrain was rolling and more thickly grown with grass and mesquite and an occasional clump of oak or cottonwood, but here along the verge of the rocky hills the ground was still semibarren. He lifted his eyes to the horizon. Mountains shimmered in the distance there, higher than the hills at his back and covered with pines.

His face set in a taut mask, Stark glanced at the nearby ground. He looked from one side of the canyon to the other, but nowhere did he find any tracks. From the looks of it, the outlaws had entered the canyon on the far side of the hills and then disappeared somewhere between here and there.

The sides of the canyon were not so steep that they couldn't be climbed. It would be difficult in most places, and the bandits would have had to lead their horses instead of ride them, but Stark was fairly certain that was what they had done. Again they had eluded pursuit, and he had no way of knowing which direction they had taken.

But he wasn't going to turn around and ride back to Buffalo Flat. He couldn't. Giving up now would be dishonoring Laura's memory, he told himself, no matter how hopeless the pursuit looked.

Stark swung down from the saddle, let the Appaloosa graze a little on the cheat grass, then poured water from his canteen into his hat and gave the horse a drink. Finding a good-sized rock on which to sit, he gnawed on some jerky and a hard biscuit he took from his saddlebags, washing the meal down with more water from the canteen. He was a man who liked to eat, as his ample stomach attested to, but his appetite seemed to have deserted him now. He ate just so he would have the strength to keep going, to keep searching for some sign of Laura's killers.

When he and the horse were both rested, Stark mounted up again and got ready to ride. He looked both north and south, intending to ride alongside the hills for a time and trying to decide which direction to try first.

The sight of a thread of smoke climbing into the sky to the south made up his mind for him.

Stark frowned and leaned forward in the saddle when he spotted the smoke. Looking back into the hills, he tried to figure the angles and decided the smoke he saw now was coming from the same place as the night before. It didn't have to mean a damned thing, of course, but his curiosity was aroused. He pointed the Appaloosa's head south and heeled the horse into a trot.

The smoke was coming from a spot at the very edge of the hills. It took Stark almost an hour to reach it. When he did, he saw that the smoke originated from the chimney of a squatty log building at the base of a steep bluff. The building was larger than a prospector or farmer would have required, and it had a hitchrack out front at which half a dozen horses were tied. Stark reined in and frowned. He had never been through these parts himself or heard anyone mention a saloon over here, but that was what he took the place to be. If there had been an actual road instead of a faint trail, the building could have been called a roadhouse. Located where it was, however, the establishment couldn't depend on passing traffic for its business. Customers would have to make a special trip to reach it.

Well, sitting out here and pondering matters wasn't going to get him any information, Stark told himself. He clucked to the Appaloosa and rode slowly toward the isolated building.

Whoever had built the place had built it to last, using thick logs that must have been freighted in from the mountains to the west. A narrow porch made of puncheons ran along the front of the building, and at one end was the massive stone chimney from which the smoke was climbing. Stark drew rein in front of the hitchrack, dismounted, and tied the Appaloosa with the other horses. Out of habit he glanced at the brands on the other animals. Without exception they were of the Mexican "skillet of snakes" variety, a meaningless jumble of lines put on with a running iron, usually to obscure whatever the original brand had been. The sight didn't make Stark feel any better about what he was walking into.

On the other hand, if this was a hideout, a stop on the so-called outlaw trail, the men he was looking for might be inside. Failing that, he might be able to get a line on them here. All he had to do was watch his back like a hawk and not say anything to tip off the customers that he was on the side of the law.

The heavy front door hung on leather hinges. Stark pushed it open and stepped inside, pausing briefly on the threshold to let his eyes adjust to the dimness. The building had only a few windows and they were covered with so much grime that barely any light was admitted.

A man yelled, "Watch out! Kill that son of a bitch!"

Stark didn't have time to let his eyes adjust or even to think about what was going on. He ducked instinctively, his hand going to the butt of the LeMat on his hip. To his left a gun boomed, deafeningly loud in the close confines of the low-ceilinged room. Stark twisted toward the sound, feeling the wind of the bullet's passage on his bearded cheek but unable to hear its whine as the place echoed with the blast of the gunshot. He had seen the flash of powder from the corner of his eye as the gun went off, and he aimed for that spot as he triggered the LeMat.

More guns crashed, this time from the opposite side of the room. The fire was returned, and Stark felt a tug on the tail of his duster and knew it was from a bullet. The part of his brain still working clamored a warning. He had just walked right into the middle of a gunfight, and he had no idea who was involved.

The folks to his right seemed to be shooting at somebody else, while at least some of the guns going off to the left were aimed at him. He squeezed off another shot at a shadowy shape on that side of the room as a hot finger of lead touched his right ear. Grimacing, Stark fired again and then again and was now left with one shot in the upper barrel of the LeMat. He didn't want to use the bottom barrel unless he had to, because the shotgun shell in it would spread buckshot indiscriminately all over that end of the room if he did.

Stark held his fire when he realized that the rest of the shooting had stopped. His ears were ringing so loudly that it took him a few seconds to recognize the silence for what it was. His nose stung from the haze of powder smoke in the room, obscuring things even more. The door had swung shut of its own accord behind him, and now he used the back of a booted foot to kick it open once more. Sunlight spilled into the tavern.

"Good thing you came in when you did, mister," a voice said from his right. "Possum and his boys had the drop on us. They'd've ventilated us for sure if you hadn't come in and spooked 'em."

The powder smoke was drifting out through

the open door now. Stark took a deep breath of the freshening air and started reloading the LeMat as he looked around. Two men stood beside an overturned table to the right, while to the left were sprawled four bodies. Stark figured he had downed at least one of them.

He hoped they had deserved killing. There hadn't been time for him to do anything else. Of course, it was pretty damned likely that anybody who would be drinking in a place like this wouldn't be any sort of hothouse flower. He looked over at the survivors and said with a grin, "Proddy sons o' bitches, weren't they?"

The man who had spoken before now laughed. "We used to run with Possum's bunch, but there was bad blood between us over a bank job down in Texas. Possum got it in his head we'd tried to cheat him out of more'n our fair share. Wasn't a lick of truth to it, of course, but nobody could talk to Possum." The man holstered his still-smoking gun and strode toward Stark, hand outstretched. "Name's Brody Cunningham. This here's my brother Anse."

Stark shook hands with the Cunningham brothers, both of whom were in their twenties, rawboned young men with dirty blond hair. They were dressed much like Stark, in well-worn range clothes, long dusters, and battered hats. Several days' worth of beard stubble and red-rimmed eyes told Stark they had been riding hard. Everything about them said outlaw.

A look at the dead men told much the same

story. Stark had blundered into a feud among thieves, and he was very lucky he was still alive, he knew.

Something round and shining in the sunlight rose on the other side of the crude bar, and after a second Stark recognized it as a man's bald head. The gent said angrily, "I've told you before, Brody—I don't like gunplay in here. You and Possum could've taken it outside."

"Shut up, Kilroy," Brody said without much real heat. "Possum never gave us no chance 'fore he threw down on us. Besides, you knew him and his boys were in here drinkin'. Why didn't you give us the high sign soon's we came in, so Anse and me could've ducked out the way we came?"

"Didn't see you in time," growled the man called Kilroy. He wore a dirty white shirt and a frayed string tie, and Stark took him for the proprietor of this place. Kilroy was a big man, broad through the shoulders with arms like an ape's, but Stark could tell from the way he licked his lips nervously when he glanced toward the dead men that he didn't have much stomach for gunplay. Kilroy would be tough enough to keep order as long as his customers were just interested in brawling, but he was the sort who would hit the floor behind the bar at the first whiff of powder smoke.

Stark slid the LeMat back into its holster. The fight was over for the time being. The Cunninghams didn't know him, but they knew he had just sided with them in the gun battle, and that was enough. After the overturned table had been set upright again, Anse called to him, "Come over here and have a drink with us, stranger, whilst Kilroy drags them corpses out back for the buzzards."

Stark knew the idea of burying the dead men would be hooted down, so he didn't even mention it. Instead he accepted Anse's invitation. He'd gotten mixed up in this trouble by accident, but that was no reason he couldn't take advantage of the unexpected development.

For all Stark knew, Brody and Anse might be two of the men he was looking for. He had never gotten close enough to any of the gang to get a good look at them as they'd looted the overturned stagecoach. But even if these two hadn't been involved in the robbery of the Whitehorse-to-Buffalo Flat stage, they might have heard about it and know who was.

Take it slow and easy, Stark warned himself. He couldn't let them have any idea who he really was or what he was really after. Their gratitude for the help he had given them would disappear instantly if they knew the truth.

"Name's Earl," he said as he looked across the table at Brody and Anse, "and that drink sounds like a mighty fine idea."

Brody signaled to Kilroy, and the tavern's proprietor brought a fresh bottle and glasses to replace the ones that had fallen on the floor when the table had turned over. Then Kilroy got busy dragging out the bodies of the outlaw called Possum and his companions.

When the drinks had been poured, Brody lifted his glass and said, "Here's to you, Earl. We'd likely be dead now if it wasn't for you."

Stark nodded in agreement and said with a smile, "Likely." He tossed off the drink, managing not to wince as the homemade brew burned its way down his gullet. He hoped old Kilroy hadn't tossed too many rattlesnake heads into the tub when he was making the stuff.

Anse licked his lips and said, "Mighty tasty. What brings you over this way, Earl? Don't reckon I've ever seen you around these parts before."

"Just drifting," replied Stark. "Trying to find some place where I can maybe lie low for a spell."

Brody laughed. "This is a good spot for that. Not many hombres wearin' badges come through these hills. Stage line passes a good way to the east, and there's nothing to the west until you get to the foothills of the mountains. There're a few settlements over there, but nobody bothers us around here. Kilroy's got the only place where you can get a drink within fifty miles."

Stark nodded, deep in thought but trying not to show it. As he had suspected, this saloon was a robbers' roost of sorts. Nobody would stop here except men on the dodge.

And that was exactly the sort he was looking for.

He knew that he had the look of a hardcase

himself, so he reinforced the image by growling, "Doesn't appear to be much for a man to do around here. No banks close by or anything like that. What's a fella supposed to do for *dinero*?"

"Best have plenty when you come," Anse told him. "Nobody works much around here. This is a place to come *after* you done a job, understand?"

Stark understood, all right.

Brody added, "And if you're runnin' a little short, or if you just feel the itch, there's always those stagecoaches runnin' north and south between Whitehorse and Buffalo Flat."

Stark's insides twisted in knots at the casual way Brody talked about holding up stagecoachs, but he kept his temper in check and maintained the pose he had adopted. "I reckon a man could make a pretty good haul from those coaches," he said as he poured himself another drink from the dark brown bottle.

"I suppose." Brody shrugged. "Anse and me, we've never been partial to things like that. We'd rather hit a bank or a train."

Stark detected a certain element of boasting to the man's talk. Ever since Frank and Jesse James had gotten so famous, it was considered somehow more glamorous to rob a train or blow up the safe in a bank. Stagecoach robberies, while still lucrative, didn't make a man famous unless he had some other sort of gimmick, like that Black Bart fella out in California, who always left behind a bit of doggerel with his victims. Stark had worked in California for a while, but he'd never run up against Bart.

Stark inclined his head toward the doorway, where Kilroy was hauling out the last corpse. "What about Possum and his boys? Were they partial to banks and trains, too?"

Anse and Brody both laughed. "Possum'd steal the rattle right out of a baby's carriage," Brody said. "It didn't make no never mind to him. I reckon that's one reason we quit ridin' with him. He just didn't have no class. But I ain't heard anything lately about him hittin' stagecoaches." Brody's eyes narrowed slightly. "What's it to you, Burl?"

With a casual shrug, Stark said, "Just curious. I like to know something about folks I've just had a hand in killing."

"They was doin' their best to plug you along with us," Anse said. "That's more'n enough for me to know."

"Damn right," Stark said emphatically. "And ol' Possum's dead, so who gives a damn? Shove that bottle back over here."

Brody and Anse both seemed to relax, the brief moment of suspicion forgotten. Stark bought the next bottle when the contents of the first one were gone, and that cemented the friendship. He spent the afternoon drinking with them, and by nightfall all three men were roaring drunk. A tiny portion of Stark's brain remained stone-cold sober, though, and that kept him from saying or doing anything that would make his companions realize he wasn't really one of them. Stark intended to maintain the perilous deception until he was sure it would be of no further use to him.

Eventually Brody and Anse stumbled off to sleep in one of the small rooms in the back of the building, and Kilroy asked Stark, "You want to rent a cot, too, mister?"

Stark shook his head. "Ain't used to sleeping with a roof over my head. I like to see the stars." He stood up shakily and dropped coins on the table. "Be seein' you, Kilroy."

He walked out, trying not to stagger. He had a hefty capacity for liquor, but this afternoon had strained it. Still, he was sober enough to realize that it had been a productive day. He had found a likely spot to turn up some information on the men he was looking for, and he'd made a couple of *amigos* in Anse and Brody Cunningham. At the same time he had helped make sure that four vicious outlaws wouldn't victimize anybody else. Of course, Brody and Anse were probably cold-blooded killers just like Possum and his gang, but at least they might be of some use to Stark in his quest.

He swung up onto the Appaloosa and rode several miles into the hills, finally finding a spot that suited him. As the day's light faded and the stars came out, Stark made camp in a little bowl of earth surrounded by brush. He made a fire and fried up some salt pork and soaked a couple of biscuits in the grease to soften them, then brewed a pot of coffee to wash it down and sober him up a little more. That done, he spread his blankets and rolled up snugly in them. The days were hot here in the Maricopas, but the nights could get mighty cold.

Stark's sleep was restless, but he didn't know if it was caused by the rotgut, the shoot-out, or the memories of Laura. Finally, far into the night, he slipped into a deep, exhausted slumber, and for a time, blessed oblivion claimed him.

Chapter Six

Stark stayed away from Kilroy's place the next day, holing up instead at the camp in the hills. He didn't want Brody and Anse to grow suspicious of him again, and spending too much time at the robbers' roost could tip them off. Better just to drop in from time to time, he thought, until Kilroy, Brody, Anse, and anybody else who frequented the place came to accept him as a regular. That would cut down on his chance of being recognized, too. The shotgun guard known as Big Earl was infamous among outlaws in these parts.

That became Stark's routine for the next couple of weeks. He rode over to the saloon nearly every other day, sometimes skipping two days instead of one just to vary things a mite. Kilroy got used to seeing him there. The Cunningham brothers weren't on hand every time Stark visited the saloon, but seldom was the log building empty of customers. Stark had no idea that so much outlaw traffic passed through the Maricopas. He bought drinks for most of the men who stopped at Kilroy's, and some of them seemed like pretty decent sorts, despite the fact that for one reason or another they rode the outlaw trail—men like Long Sam Littlejohn, Sonny Tabor, John

Temple, and Shade Mallory. Others, such as Jake Walsh, Pax Lorrimer, and Reb Turner, were nothing but rabid skunks in human form. Stark tried to get along with all of them as he subtly, carefully pumped them for information about a gang that preyed on the stagecoaches running through the area.

Not surprisingly, he didn't learn anything. Most outlaws were pretty closemouthed. But occasionally whiskey or a man's ego—or a combination of both—would start him to bragging, and that was where Stark held out the hope of discovering what he needed to know.

He was in Kilroy's one day, a little more than two weeks after the gunfight that had won him the gratitude and friendship of the Cunningham brothers, when three men he hadn't seen before strode into the saloon and went to the bar. One of them slapped a callused palm on the scarred wood and bellowed, "Whiskey! And we want the good bottle, goddammit, not that stuff full of strychnine and gunpowder!"

"Whiskey's whiskey," Kilroy returned in a surly voice. "Ain't but one kind around here." He reached onto a shelf behind him for a full bottle and pulled the cork.

"Lemme see that." The man reached across the bar and snatched the bottle from Kilroy's hand, lifted it to his lips, and took a long guzzle. Then in one swift movement he lowered the bottle and spewed out the liquor left in his mouth. "Gawd damn! What *is* that?"

Kilroy's beefy face was flushed with anger. "Whiskey, just like you asked for, mister. And that bottle'll cost you four bits."

The obnoxious stranger gave an arrogant laugh as he thumped the bottle down on the bar with his left hand. His right swept the gun from the holster on his hip and brought it up in a flashing movement almost too quick for the eye to follow. Before anybody else in the bar could do anything, the muzzle of the gun was gouging painfully into the soft flesh of Kilroy's neck just under his chin. The hammer of the pistol was thumbed back, ready to fall.

"Just you watch your mouth, you bald-headed bastard," growled the stranger, and his two companions chuckled at him. "That skull of yours may not be able to grow hair, but I can sure as hell cover it with blood and brains when my slug comes bustin' out the other side."

Stark was sitting at a table by himself. Half a dozen other men were in the room, but none made a move to get involved. Stark hesitated, unsure what he should do. He had no love for Kilroy—the man's business catered to outlaws and killers—but at the same time it was difficult, if not impossible, for Stark to stand aside and watch a person's brains get blown out, even a no-account like Kilroy.

Maybe he wouldn't *have* to do anything, he told himself. Maybe the newcomer was just full of piss and vinegar, anxious to show everybody how tough he was. Could be he'd just threaten Kilroy and leave it at that.

Stark hoped he guessed right. Otherwise the saloon's proprietor would die.

Abruptly the stranger let out a laugh and lowered the hammer on his six-gun. He took the barrel away from Kilroy's neck and laughed again. "Scared you, didn't I?" he asked. "I reckon you'd best go see if you got a clean pair o' pants, mister. And while you're at it, leave the bottle. We'll drink it, even if it ain't nothin' but rotgut."

"F-four bits," Kilroy said shakily.

The stranger let out a whoop and rattled a coin on the bar. "The *cojones* on you must be bigger'n a brass monkey's, I'll give you that," he said. Turning to his companions, he went on, "Let's find a place to sit down, fellas."

The crisis apparently over, Stark sipped his own drink again. He wondered who the strangers were. Desperadoes, obviously. No other kind of man ever came to Kilroy's . . . except for himself, of course. But he knew better than to think anyone else in the room was just pretending to be an outlaw.

One of the two men accompanying the proddy stranger cackled with laughter as they sat down and started passing around the bottle. "Damn, Lee Roy, I thought that fella's eyes were goin' to pop right out of his head when you shoved your hogleg in his neck."

"He did look a mite scared, didn't he?" Lee Roy asked with a sneer. He was a slender man, a little below medium height, with tangled, greasy red hair under a battered black hat. Not an impressive specimen at all, he struck Stark as the type to think that a gun in his hand made him the next thing to God. He'd be a pure bully with a coward's heart. Stark despised him on sight.

The other two were bigger and cut from the same cloth, but their dull-witted expressions revealed why Lee Roy seemed to be their leader, even though he was smaller. The redhead might not be very smart, but he could probably think rings around his partners.

Stark hitched his chair around slightly and tried to ignore them, but as they got drunker they became more raucous. He paid as little attention to them as he could, although he listened to their conversation with one ear, just out of habit. You never knew when somebody was going to say something that could turn out to be helpful.

That was why he went rigid when one of Lee Roy's companions said, "I'll bet that was the funniest thing you seen since that stagecoach you told us about went tumblin' over and over."

Stark's blood seemed to turn to ice in his veins, and a great roar of rage welled up his throat. He stopped it at the last instant before it escaped, his muscles quivering from the effort required not to stand up and hurl himself across the room at Lee Roy. He could see his fingers wrapping around the scrawny outlaw's throat, could feel bones and flesh being crushed in his grip. But that could wait—until he found out more.

Stark noticed an empty chair at the table where Lee Roy and his friends sat. Standing up, he sauntered over and put a hand on the back of the unoccupied chair. The three men gave him cold looks.

"That was a mighty hilarious show you put on, friend," he said with a grin. "I'd like to buy you a drink by way of thankin' you for the entertainment."

Lee Roy and the others relaxed slightly. "I never turn down a free drink," Lee Roy said. "Set yourself down if you're of a mind to." He paused, then added, "Ain't missed many meals in your life, have you, pard?"

Stark's grin never wavered as he said, "I've never minded what folks call me, long as they don't call me late for supper."

One of the other men laughed and slapped his denim-clad thigh. "You're a caution, ain't you, big boy?" he said.

"I try to be," Stark replied. He crooked a finger at Kilroy and called for another bottle.

Kilroy nodded. It seemed as if he didn't much want to bring it over to the table, but he did anyway. Stark tossed the man a coin, then pulled the cork with his teeth, spitting it out onto the floor before lifting the bottle and letting a big slug of the whiskey gurgle down his throat. Tears appeared in his eyes. He started the bottle circulating.

For a few minutes all four men at the table were busy with serious drinking. Then Stark wiped the back of his hand across his mouth and asked Lee Roy, "What was that you were sayin' about some stagecoach turnin' over? I'll bet that was a sight to see."

"Sure was," agreed Lee Roy. "I was ridin' with some fellas from over west of here, not a bunch I usually run with, but they was needin' some help on this job and I reckon I got lucky. Made a good haul, too, but the best part was seein' that stage and the team pullin' it go head over heels. The driver and the guard flew like birds when it went over, let me tell you. The wreck didn't kill 'em, but we took care of that in a hurry."

A pulse like the hammering of a blacksmith's anvil was sounding in Stark's head, but he managed not to show his turmoil as he said, "Sounds like my kind of hombres. You know where I could meet up with 'em?"

"Well, I tell you, big un—"

At that moment the door of the saloon opened, and Brody and Anse Cunningham stepped inside. Spotting Stark, Brody called out, "Howdy, Earl!"

One of the men with Lee Roy caught his breath sharply. "Earl!" he repeated. "Big un . . . Big Earl! I knew I seen him somewhere before! Goddammit, this is Big Earl, that shotgun guard!" With that, he sprang up so fast that his chair overturned behind him. His hand darted toward the gun on his hip.

Stark bit back a curse. He had never been a fast draw, and the other man already had his fingers wrapped around the butt of his gun. But Stark had time to grab the edge of the table and shove it at the man as hard as he could. The table caught the man in the upper thighs and knocked him backward. His gun blasted, but the slug smacked into the floor.

Already moving, Stark was on his feet even as the pistol went off. His arm swept behind him, caught the top rung of the ladder-back chair, and swung the piece of furniture up and over his head. He brought it crashing down on the skull of the second man, who was also reaching for a gun. The impact flattened the man's hat and sent him sprawling limply to the floor, out cold, the remains of the splintered chair around him.

That left Lee Roy, and Stark backhanded him as the little outlaw came up out of his chair. Lee Roy plunged backward and slumped against the bar.

"Big Earl!" somebody yelled.

Stark wheeled around. The fellow who had yelled his name might as well have signed his death warrant. Mainly because Stark had sent so many outlaws either to jail or to blazes that he wouldn't likely be welcomed by their compadres. He was lucky no one had recognized him until now, he knew.

But now it was too late, and men were jumping up all over the room and either slapping leather or charging toward him. Stark palmed out the LeMat, not blindingly fast but quick and steady, and triggered twice, sending two of the gun-toters spinning off their feet. Now that gunplay had entered the fracas, the men who had been charging him stopped and grabbed for their own hardware instead.

Stark had no choice. He pivoted the striker on the hammer as he cocked the LeMat. A couple of slugs whipped past him, but then he squeezed the trigger and touched off the .63 caliber shotgun shell in the lower barrel around which the regular cylinder rotated. The heavy boom was deafening, and the recoil from the blast surged up Stark's arm. The charge of buckshot spread out fast, ripping into the cluster of gunmen and mowing them down. Stark thumbed the hammer back into its normal position and spun toward the doorway as Brody Cunningham howled, "We trusted you, you son of a bitch!"

Both Cunninghams were pulling their guns. Because of their friendship, they had hesitated a split second while Stark dealt with the other men in the room, and that was the only thing that had saved him. He fired twice, aiming for Brody first, since Brody was faster on the draw and more dangerous. The bullet slammed into Brody's chest, knocking him backward. An instant later, Anse's pistol cracked, the report blending with Stark's second shot in a deadly harmony. Anse doubled over and crumpled as Stark's bullet took him in the belly.

Stark started breathing again. The whole gunfight had only taken seconds, but it had seemed much longer to him. He looked down at himself and decided that he hadn't been hit anywhere, which was damned lucky.

From behind him came a hideous, strangled sound. He turned, gun still in hand, to see the outlaw called Lee Roy flopping around on the floor, trying with his fingers to stem the tide of blood from his bullet-torn throat. Stark realized that Lee Roy must have been getting to his feet when Anse Cunningham's shot had missed Stark and hit him instead. Stark went to one knee beside the little outlaw, all too aware that Lee Roy held the key to finding the other men who had taken part in the holdup that took Laura's life. Ignoring the blood, he gripped Lee Roy's shoulder and shouted, "Don't die, damn you! Don't die! Tell me about that stage robbery. Who was in on it with you?"

Lee Roy gave a huge shudder, and a fresh gout of blood welled through the fingers around his throat. An ugly gurgle was the only sound that came from his open mouth. His feet beat an urgent tattoo on the floor as he died.

Stark's gaze switched to the two men who had entered Kilroy's with the dead outlaw. Neither of them moved as they lay sprawled on the floor. The skull of the one Stark had hit over the head with the chair was flattened and knocked out of shape, and Stark knew he was dead. So was the other one, due to a couple of bullet holes in his chest, Stark discovered a moment later. Stray slugs must have gotten to him, too, just like Lee Roy.

Stark cursed bitterly. He wished that somebody who could tell him where to find Laura's murderers was still alive. But it was possible that Lee Roy had told him enough before all hell broke loose.

Stark stood up, reloaded the LeMat, and walked around the room to check on the other men. Some were dead, while others were unconscious. He intended to be well away from here before any of the survivors regained their senses.

Stark turned toward the bar. No one stood behind it. He bellowed, "Kilroy!"

Not surprisingly, the owner of the robbers' roost was still alive. Stark reckoned he had ducked down out of harm's way at the first sign of trouble. Now Kilroy asked, without lifting himself off the floor, "What the hell do you want?" You've already shot up my place!"

"What's west of here?"

The question made Kilroy curious enough to rise up and peer over the bar with a frown. "What?"

"West of here," Stark repeated. "There are settlements over that way. What's the closest one?"

"There's a place in the foothills called Ryanville. Nothing much between here and there, I don't reckon." Kilroy glanced around wide-eyed at the carnage. "You killed 'em all!"

"Just most of them," replied Stark. He lifted the LeMat and lined its barrel on Kilroy's pasty face. "You didn't know that bastard called Lee Roy, did you?"

Kilroy swallowed hard and answered, "Never saw him before today. If he rode in from the west, though, he could've come from Ryanville. There's sure as hell nothing between here and there."

Stark lowered the gun. The information wasn't much, but it was all he had and better than nothing. He was sure that Lee Roy was one of the men who had held up the stage to Buffalo Flat. But the outlaw had said that he wasn't a regular member of the gang, which left plenty of questions unanswered.

Maybe the answers could be found in Ryanville, Stark thought. He holstered his gun and strode out of Kilroy's place without looking back. Jerking loose the Appaloosa's reins, he swung up into the saddle and headed west. The sun was low in the sky, but he could still cover some ground before it got dark, and maybe by morning he'd be that much closer to the men he intended to find.

Chapter Seven

Stark rode into Ryanville in the early evening of the second day after leaving Kilroy's place. The saloonkeeper had been telling the truth—there wasn't much between the two places. Stark had seen a few cattle as he rode across the rolling plains toward the mountains, and that meant at least one ranch was in the area, but he hadn't seen any buildings or roaming cowboys. Except for coyotes, jackrabbits, ground squirrels, and an occasional deer bounding along in the distance, he seemed to be alone in the vast landscape.

Stark was accustomed to being by himself, though, and the loneliness didn't bother him as much as it might have a city fellow who was used to clamor and crowds around him all the time. To Stark it was just peaceful, and the ride gave him time to think.

The bandits who had held up the stage had to have some sort of home base. Loot didn't do anybody a damned bit of good without a place to spend it. So it was reasonable to think that between jobs they holed up somewhere, and the settlement called Ryanville was as good a place as any to start looking for them.

The terrain grew more rugged as he approached the foothills, pines replacing the mesquite and scrub oaks of the lower elevations. At dusk Stark spotted the lights of the settlement up ahead and felt his pulse quicken.

Laura's killers could be up there, secure in a room lit by the warm yellow glow of a lamp, counting the money they had stolen. The idea filled Stark with rage.

Soon enough, he thought. Soon enough they would get what was coming to them. Only it wouldn't be, not really. It could never be soon enough for Laura. . . .

Ryanville sat in a valley between two thickly wooded hills. At the far end of its main street was a wooden bridge over a creek that ran down from the hill to the north. The settlement was bigger than Stark had expected. He'd figured it would be nothing more than a wide place in the trail, maybe with a saloon, trading post, and a couple of houses but little else. Instead he found himself riding down the main street of a good-sized small town. The business district was four blocks long, and several dozen houses were scattered around on cross streets.

The first business Stark came to as he rode into town was a livery stable, a big barn on his left. The lantern that hung over the open double doors was already lit, and a man sat in a chair beside the doors, reading. Stark veered toward him. As he approached, he saw that the gaudy-jacketed publication in the man's hands was a dime novel.

"Howdy, mister," the man greeted Stark. The

chair in which he sat was tilted back against the wall of the barn, but he leaned forward and let the front legs thump down. Folding the dime novel, he stuck it in the hip pocket of his denim pants as he stood up. "Something I can do for you?"

"Got a vacant stall for my horse?" Stark asked without dismounting.

The man's head bobbed up and down. "Sure do. We don't get that many pilgrims through Ryanville, and there's always a couple of empty stalls. Cost you two bits. That includes a rubdown and a good graining."

"Sounds fine to me," Stark said as he swung down from the saddle. He handed the Appaloosa's reins to the liveryman.

Now that he had gotten a better look, Stark realized that the hostler was young, probably no more than twenty or so. He had dark hair under his floppy-brimmed hat, and his eyes shone with intelligence and alertness. He gave Stark a friendly grin as he patted the Appaloosa's shoulder and said, "Mighty fine-looking horse."

"He is," Stark agreed. "Take good care of him."

"Oh, I can promise you I will, Mr. . . .?"

"Stark." The reply came after a second's hesitation. Maybe nobody here in Ryanville knew him or had heard of him.

"Glad to meet you, Mr. Stark. They call me the Kid."

A grin tugged at Stark's mouth. It seemed as

if half the youngsters in the West fed their dreams of gunfighting glory with a steady diet of dime-novel exploits, and most of them called themselves Kid Something-or-other or So-and-So the Kid. At least this one appeared to be unarmed. Too many carried around rusty old pistols that were just as likely to blow up in their hands as to fire, and they got themselves killed with alarming regularity by picking fights. Stark hoped that this particular Kid had more sense than that.

Looking up and down the street, Stark tried without much success in the fading light to read the signs on the buildings. He could make out the leading saloon easily enough, catty-cornered across the street from the livery stable. The big, false-fronted frame building had large windows and a batwinged door through which spilled light and music and raucous laughter. A couple of smaller buildings down the street were also brightly lit, and Stark figured them to be less opulent saloons. Other than that, thought, he wasn't sure where anything was located.

"Reckon you could point my way to the local deputy's office?" he asked the young hostler.

The Kid laughed. "Deputy? There's no lawman in Ryanville, Mr. Stark, not even a town marshal."

Stark frowned and said, "You mean the county sheriff doesn't keep a man down here in case of trouble?"

"I guess he doesn't think it'd be worthwhile.

This is a pretty peaceful place, even without a badgetoter."

His broad shoulders lifting in a shrug, Stark said, "Hope it stays that way." He pushed back his duster, hooked his left thumb in his shell belt, and rubbed at his bearded jaw with his right hand. He had intended to ask the local lawman about any strangers who might have ridden through in recent weeks. One of the five men who had held up the stage was back there at Kilroy's place, dead. Stark was sure of that. But there were four more left, four men he had to find.

He turned his attention back to the Kid. "You work here at the stable most of the time?"

"Spend just about all my days and nights here," replied the youngster. "Old Mr. Jenks, who owns the place, ain't as spry as he used to be, so I handle the chores. He pays me a good wage and lets me sleep in the tack room."

"So you see everybody who comes and goes, is that right?"

The Kid grinned. "Pert' near. I sit out here most of the time when I'm not working inside."

"Think back over the last couple of weeks." Stark was going to take a shot in the dark. The Kid seemed bright and alert, and he was in a good position to have seen anything important. "Have you seen four men, strangers most likely, riding in and out of town?"

"Four men? What do they look like?"

Stark shook his head. "Wish I could tell you, but I don't rightly know. All I'm sure of is that there were four of them and they were wearing long dusters, sort of like mine."

The Kid's eyes lit up, and for an instant Stark felt a surge of anticipation, thinking that his description had rung a bell in the hostler's brain. But then the Kid said, "I don't recollect seeing anybody like that, Mr. Stark, but all these questions have got me curious. You're some kind of lawman, ain't you?"

The Kid was a little sharper than Stark had expected. And he could tell from the excited look on the young man's face that more of those dime-novel dreams were percolating inside his brain. The Kid probably figured that Stark was a U.S. marshal or a Pinkerton, and Stark could almost hear him volunteering to be his unofficial assistant. Best to nip that idea in the bud.

"Hell, no, I'm no star-packer," he said bluntly. "I'm just looking for those gents because I've got business with 'em. Business of my own," he added with a meaningful frown.

With a crestfallen look the Kid nodded. "Sorry. Didn't mean to go poking around in other folks' affairs. Wish I could help you, Mr. Stark, but the only stranger I know of in Ryanville is that hombre right over there." The Kid lifted a hand and pointed toward the saloon across the street. "He's been around town for about a week."

Stark saw a well-built man of medium height walking toward the entrance of the saloon. The man sported a short dark beard and wore a dark Stetson with silver conchos on the band, as well as a black duster somewhat shorter than the one Stark wore. The coat was pushed back on his right to reveal the walnut butt of a holstered Colt.45, and something about the way the man carried himself as he pushed through the batwings and entered the saloon told Stark that he knew how to use the weapon.

Stark frowned. The duster was different from the type worn by the outlaws during the holdup, but a man could change his clothes, couldn't he? With some gangs, like Frank and Jesse and their pards, the dusters were almost a uniform, and it made sense that if some hombres were lying low they'd go to some pains to change their appearance. And just because this man was alone didn't mean that he wasn't part of the bunch Stark was looking for.

Those thoughts raced through Stark's mind in an instant, and he knew he had to follow up on them, even if nothing came of it. He slapped the Appaloosa on the rump and said, "I could use a drink and something to eat, too, just like this old boy. I'll leave him with you." He tossed a two-bit piece to the Kid, who deftly plucked the spinning coin out of the air.

"Thanks, Mr. Stark. Like I said, I'll take good care of your horse." The young man smiled as he went on, "And if you need a good rubdown with your drink and feedbag, like this here Appaloosa, you go right on over there to Doc Teague's place. He's got some really pretty gals working for him."

Stark chuckled. "Know that for a fact, do you?"

The Kid had the good grace to blush in the lantern light. "Well, that's what I've heard, anyway."

Stark gave the youngster a wave and ambled across the street toward the saloon. As he got closer, he could make out the writing on the false front over the entrance: TEAGUE'S ACE-HIGH SALOON, it said.

Stark could tell the place was doing a good business even before he reached the boardwalk in front of it. Judging from the amount of noise coming from inside, Teague's was a popular establishment here in Ryanville. Stark stepped up onto the boardwalk and crossed the planks to the entrance, pausing with his hands on top of the batwings before he swung them open.

There was a smell that all saloons had, a mixture of whiskey and beer, tobacco smoke, cheap perfume, and human sweat. Stark had spent countless nights smelling that smell, and it filled his nostrils now as he moved slowly into the Ace-High. The layout was similar to that of many other saloons he had been in: to the right a long mahogany bar with a brass rail at its foot, in the center of the room tables for drinking and gambling, and to the left a small raised platform with a piano. At the left rear of the room was a staircase leading up to a narrow balcony, and opening off it were half a dozen doors. The rooms up there would be small, little more than cubbyholes with beds, since it was more of a loft than a second floor, just some space stolen from the high-ceilinged main room so that the saloon girls would have a place to ply their trade.

Behind the bar was a large mirror and several shelves lined with bottles. The opposite wall on both sides of the piano platform was adorned with stuffed and mounted animal heads—deer, antelope, moose, mountain lion—along with an impressive pair of antlers and a large buffalo skull. The big room was lit by three oil-burning chandeliers, which added to the blue-gray haze of smoke.

In the saloon were at least two dozen customers, a mixture of cowboys and townies. Several gaudily garbed young women moved among them, serving drinks, chatting, and generally flirting. A couple of card games were going on. The piano was silent at the moment, with no piano player in sight, so nobody was dancing. But it was early yet.

Stark spotted the man who had been pointed out to him by the Kid. The stranger was standing at the bar nursing a beer. On the other side of the bar was an attractive woman wearing a frilly long-sleeved blouse that buttoned up to her neck. Her dark hair was worn short, cut in a simple but appealing style. She had a dazzling smile as she talked to the stranger.

"Why, it's nice of you to say such things, Mr. Pollard," the woman was saying as Stark sidled up to the bar a few places away from the man in the black duster. "Doc and I are very proud of

115

the Ace-High. You won't find a better saloon anywhere in the territory."

"I'm sure of that," replied the stranger called Pollard.

"If I can get you anything else, you just let me know." With that, the woman turned away from Pollard and drifted down the bar toward Stark. She gave him the same smile and asked, "And what can I do for you, mister?"

"Beer'd be fine," Stark told her. Obviously she was the proprietor of this place, along with somebody called Doc who was probably her husband. Otherwise she wouldn't be working behind the bar like this. Stark watched as she filled a mug with beer from a keg below the bar, then slid it across to him. "Much obliged."

"You're welcome. And welcome to Ryanville. I don't believe I've seen you around before."

"Just rode into town a few minutes ago," Stark said, not offering any more information.

"Are you here on business? Staying long or just passing through?"

The woman was a mite more inquisitive than most bartenders, Stark thought. But he didn't want to be impolite, so he just said, "Passing through, I imagine," and ignored the question about whether or not business had brought him here.

"Well, we appreciate your stopping in." She added almost apologetically, "The beer is seventy-five cents."

Six bits was much higher than normal for a

glass of beer, but Stark could understand that, given Ryanville's isolated location. He took coins from the pocket of his denim pants and slid them across the bar.

"If there's anything else I can do for you, just let me know," the woman said as she picked up the money. "My name is Belle."

Stark lifted his mug in a half-salute. "Pleased to meet you, ma'am."

Belle moved on to some of the other customers, working the bar smoothly and professionally. There was another bartender, a balding drink-juggler in an apron, white shirt, and string tie, and Stark noticed that he did most of the actual work while Belle did the glad-handing of customers and poured only an occasional drink. A beautiful woman like her behind the bar would be a drawing card for the saloon, though, no matter how much work she did.

Stark spent the next few minutes sipping his beer, which was both cold and good, keeping an eye on the rest of the room by watching the big mirror behind the bar. There was a little traffic up and down the stairs, the saloon girls in their brightly colored dresses arm in arm with the cowboys and tradesmen who patronized the place. That confirmed Stark's guess about what went on up there in those little rooms.

"Hello, Dan!"

The friendly voice to Stark's left drew his attention, and he glanced in that direction to see one of the saloon girls greeting Pollard by throwing her bare arms around his neck and kissing him soundly. The young woman had curly, light brown hair and a slender figure, which she showed off to advantage in a low-cut red dress with a fringed hem high enough to display most of her stunning legs. She pushed herself brazenly against Pollard, who responded by looping an arm around her trim waist and pulling her even closer.

"Howdy, Dinah," Stark heard him say when the kiss was over. "Where've you been keeping yourself this evening?"

"Why, waiting for you, of course, sugar. I didn't think you were ever going to come back and see me again." She pouted insincerely but prettily.

Pollard laughed and swatted her lightly on the rump. "Sure," he said. "You knew good and well I couldn't stay away too long, Dinah."

Pollard had obviously made a conquest in the time he had been in Ryanville. Of course, a girl like Dinah would be friendly with anybody who could afford to pay for her time, but from the way she was treating Pollard, Stark figured he not only had money, and plenty of it, but was willing to spend it as well.

Maybe that money was part of the shipment stolen from the stagecoach, Stark thought. With a share of that loot, Pollard could afford to be a free spender.

But he was getting ahead of himself, the big man thought. His study of the law books and the short time he had spent as a practicing attorney had taught him about things such as evidence and the idea that a man was innocent until proven guilty. Pollard could be here in Ryanville for any number of reasons, just as there would be more than one explanation for his having plenty of money in his pocket. Stark cautioned himself to be patient and not jump to conclusions.

Still, his years of experience as a shotgun guard had also taught him a few things, and one was when to be suspicious of a fellow. When he looked at Dan Pollard, every instinct in Stark's body warned him that here was a man with something to hide.

Pollard and Dinah talked for several more minutes, the conversation animated and friendly. With all the other talk and laughter in the room, Stark could make out some of their words, but not all. What he heard, however, seemed innocuous enough, the kind of banter that a man would exchange with a girl in Dinah's line of work before he took her upstairs. Pollard bought another beer and bought Dinah a drink as well, which was poured by the male bartender. Belle was down at the other end of the bar, talking to a couple of gents in town clothes. Stark looked at the pale amber liquid in Dinah's glass and guessed it wasn't anything stronger than tea, although Pollard would have paid for something more expensive. That was a standard dodge in places like this; everybody was aware of it, and nobody seemed to mind.

After a few more minutes, Pollard put his arm around Dinah's waist again and leaned close to nuzzle her neck. She threw back her head and laughed. Then Pollard put his lips next to her ear and whispered a question. She nodded, and together they turned away from the bar and started toward the narrow stairway.

Stark swallowed the rest of his beer to hide the grimace that passed across his face as Pollard and Dinah climbed the stairs. Nothing he had seen or heard here in the Ace-High had lessened his suspicions about Pollard. He was still intensely curious about the man. But there were limits to how far eavesdropping could be carried. Until Pollard came back downstairs of his own accord, Stark was stuck down here.

"Another beer, fella?" asked the bartender, noticing that Stark's mug was empty.

Stark hesitated, but only for a second, before nodding and shoving the empty glass across the bar. The bartender refilled it and collected the coins that Stark offered. The gent wasn't nearly as friendly—or as pretty—as Belle, but he was efficient enough; Stark had to give him that.

Stark picked up the beer and turned around, hooking a bootheel on the brass rail and leaning back against the bar. He let his eyes scan the room, and his gaze fell on one of the tables where a poker game was under way. A hand had just ended, and a man in a black coat and fancy vest was leaning forward to rake in the pot as the other players registered reactions ranging from good-natured disappointment to outright disgust at their bad luck. One of them shook his head and stood up. "I'm out, boys," Stark heard him say. "I'm a poor man, and this game's too rich for my blood."

The man was well dressed and looked as if he could still afford to lose a few hands, but some hombres couldn't stand a steady diet of losing no matter how flush they were. The player's departure left an empty chair at the table, and acting on a whim, Stark walked over, carrying his beer.

Chapter Eight

Looks like you fellas need another player," Stark said as the winner of the previous hand began shuffling the cards with the practiced ease of a professional gambler.

"New blood is always welcome," the man said with a ready grin. "Sit yourself down, my friend. We're playing five-card stud. That suit your fancy?"

"Just fine," Stark said as he settled himself into the vacant chair.

The dealer extended a hand with long, slender fingers and said, "I'm Doc Teague. This place belongs to my wife and me."

"Lady at the bar named Belle?"

"That's right," Doc said.

"Fine lady. My name's Stark." He shook hands with Doc.

The gambler was in his midforties, with sandy hair starting to turn gray, keen blue eyes, and the quick grin that had greeted Stark. He introduced the other four men around the table, Russell, Niebuhr, Nevins, and Pachter, and Stark filed away their names in his mind, even though all of them looked like upstanding citizens of Ryanville with no connection to the holdup that had brought him here. Nobody was completely above suspicion, though, and that was the way it would be until Stark had completed his mission.

Doc had the biggest pile of money in front of him. In a lot of places the fact that the house was the big winner might have led to angry words or even gunplay, but Doc's jovial manner seemed to make the losers not mind so much. Stark hoped that continued; he wanted to kill some time in a friendly game while he was waiting for Pollard and Dinah to get through upstairs.

The ante was two bits. Stark bought in and studied the cards that Doc flipped deftly around the table. He kept one eye on the cards and one on the stairs as the hand got under way, hoping he wasn't being too obvious.

Nobody around the table seemed to notice that he was preoccupied. The betting came to a head quickly, and the man named Nevins won the hand with three kings. Doc got the cards back with the next hand, taking it with a full house. Stark lost a little both times, but not enough to bother him.

The talk was as enjoyable as the card-playing. Although all of the men were friendly and gregarious, Doc seemed to be the most talkative. Stark decided to take advantage of that by saying, "This is my first visit to Ryanville. I wasn't expecting such a big place. Get many travelers coming through here?"

Doc shook his head. "Not really. Most folks are pretty well settled and have been here awhile. There are quite a few ranches to the north of here, along the foothills of the mountains, so I reckon that's why the town grew up. There's no railroad or stage line, though, nor any main roads coming through here, so I reckon Ryanville's about as big as it's going to get."

"Which suits us just fine," one of the other players said. "It's a nice peaceful place to live and raise up a family."

Stark understood the sentiment. Out here on the frontier, there was a constant conflict of emotions where progress and growth were concerned. Civilization was fine and dandy, but too much of it brought problems. The citizens of Ryanville no doubt appreciated its being tucked away here at the edge of nowhere.

"I reckon I must be the first stranger to come through here in a while," Stark commented idly, "judging by the way you boys are talking."

"Not really," Doc replied. "There's a fella named Pollard . . . Shoot, he was at the bar a few minutes ago. Where'd he get off to? Anyway, he's a newcomer, too. I think everybody at the table would agree he's not near as friendly as you, Mr. Stark."

"That's right," said Niebuhr. "He's been in a couple of fights already with some cowboys. I don't like drifters like that. There's always a chance the man could turn out to be some kind of hardcase."

"Fights about what?" Stark asked.

Russell laughed. "A woman, what else? Pollard seems to think he's got first claim on Dinah."

"Well, he's got plenty of money to spend on her," Doc said. "That only goes so far, though. I won't tolerate a man who makes trouble, no matter how much money he has in his pocket."

Stark nodded and sipped his beer. "I'm a peaceable man, myself," he said.

"And I could tell that about you right away, Mr. Stark." Doc grinned and dealt the cards again.

Stark leaned back and pondered the things he had just heard concerning Dan Pollard. He was a rough customer, and he wasn't hurting for cash, just the sort of man Stark was looking for. He was a stranger in Ryanville, to boot.

Stark let the play proceed for a while, then asked casually, "Any other towns around here?"

"There's a place called Cross Cut west of here in the mountains," Doc answered, "and down south you've got Tin Top and Waverly. None of them are as big as Ryanville, but I reckon they're nice enough towns if you're looking for a place to settle down. I'd recommend our own little community, though."

"Don't reckon I'm looking to put down roots just yet," Stark said with a shake of his head. "Just curious, since I've never been through these parts before."

"You haven't said what brings you this way, Mr. Stark," one of the other players commented.

"That's right, I haven't." Out of habit, Stark's tone was a little cool.

Doc said smoothly, "I'm sure Josh didn't mean

any offense, Mr. Stark. You've noticed yourself that we don't have many newcomers around here, so we're naturally curious."

Stark smiled. "No offense taken." The others might be waiting for him to fill in more of his background, but they were going to be disappointed. He changed the subject by turning over the cards in his hand and saying, "I'll fold."

The game continued. Stark drank a few more beers and between hands visited the bar long enough to pick up some ham, boiled eggs, and crackers from the free food tray. Almost before he knew it, several hours had passed, and he was down about thirty dollars in the game, most of it lost to Doc Teague.

Not only that, but Pollard and Dinah had still not reappeared, and Stark had concluded they wouldn't be down anytime soon. If Pollard had plenty of money, there was no reason the man couldn't have paid for the whole night with Dinah. It might be better to wait for another night to find out more about him. Stark was in no hurry; he could afford to spend some time in Ryanville.

For a change Stark won the next hand, recouping about half of his losses. He pulled in the money and said, "Well, I think winning that hand must have been an omen. I'm going to call it a night."

Doc grinned at him. "Most men would see winning as a sign their luck had changed, Mr.

Stark. Maybe you can win more if you stay with it."

Stark shook his head. "If my luck's really changed, it'll still be good tomorrow night. Reckon there'll be a game then, too?"

"There's always a game," Doc said. "I take it you're staying a day or two?"

"I think I will. Town seems mighty hospitable."

"Then let me recommend the Moffatt Hotel across the street. The rooms are comfortable and the prices are fair."

"Can't ask for more than that," Stark said as he stood up and gathered the bills and coins in front of him. He stowed away the money inside his vest, then nodded at the other players. "Evenin', gents."

"Good evening, Mr. Stark," Doc said.

As Stark went to the door, Belle called after him from the bar, "You come back to see us!"

Stark turned and smiled at her, touching a finger to the brim of his hat. As he pushed through the batwings, he almost ran head-on into an elderly man entering the saloon. He was a little taller than Stark, with the weathered features and lean, whipcord-and-whang-leather build of an hombre who had spent his life working hard. His white hair stuck out from a battered old black hat.

"'Scuse me, mister," the man said. "Didn't mean to run into you."

"That's all right, Pops," Stark told him. "No harm done."

The old man gave Stark a puzzled frown. "How'd you know my name?" he asked.

"You mean Pops? Well . . ." Suddenly Stark felt a little embarrassed. He'd had no right to be disrespectful of the old man. He finished lamely, "A lucky guess, I reckon."

"No need to let it bother you, son," Pops said with a grin. "I'm just the swamper here. No reason to worry 'bout hurtin' my feelings."

Stark gave him a curt nod and moved on, stepping onto the boardwalk as the swamper went inside the saloon. The night was warm, and Stark drew in a deep lungful of the fresh air outside the Ace-High. After a brief pause, he started across the street toward a two-story white frame structure with several lights burning in its windows. That would be the Moffatt Hotel, he figured.

The affable, middle-aged clerk behind the desk in the hotel lobby checked him in and gave him a room on the second floor front, which was all right with Stark. He planned to keep an eye on the Ace-High for a while before turning in, just in case Pollard came out. Lightly bouncing the room key on the palm of his hand, Stark went up the broad staircase.

The upper hallway was lit by lamps at each end, but the middle section was fairly dim. Still, Stark had no trouble finding his room. He put the key in the lock and turned it.

No one in Ryanville knew him except the youngster at the livery stable and the people he had met earlier in the saloon, so Stark wasn't being particularly careful as he opened the door and stepped into the darkened room. His experience as a stagecoach guard had given him the habit of caution, however, and he reacted instantly when he sensed someone in the room. His hand dipped toward the LeMat on his hip, even as he wished he had his greener. But the scattergun was still on his saddle, back at the livery stable with the Appaloosa.

"Hold it right there, mister!" a voice ordered sharply, and the command was punctuated by a sound Stark knew all too well—the hammer of a pistol being drawn back. He froze where he was, his fingers still an inch from the butt of the LeMat. The door was open behind him, and even though the light in the hall was dim, it was more than enough to make his silhouetted form an easy target, especially since he filled up most of the doorway. For an instant Stark thought about flinging himself to one side and making a try for the LeMat anyway, but he quickly gave up the idea. At this range it was damned near impossible to jump out of the way of a cocked and aimed gun.

Besides, he had recognized the voice of the intruder, and he wanted to know how the hell the very man he'd been wanting to see had ended up here in his hotel room, waiting for him with a gun.

"Shut that door behind you, but don't get any fancy ideas about jumping out into the hall," Dan Pollard said. "I can drop you before you even get started."

"I don't doubt that for a minute." Stark kept his voice cool and calm as he reached behind him to shove the door shut.

The rasp of a match sounded, and Stark squinted his eyes against the reddish glare that suddenly brightened the room. He stood motionless while Pollard held the flame to the wick of a lamp on the table beside him.

As the yellow glow of the lamplight spread through the room, Stark saw that Pollard was sitting in the only chair, his booted feet stretched out in front of him and his legs crossed at the ankles. He looked a lot more casual than he should have, considering that he had been waiting here in the dark for God knew how long, waiting for Stark with a gun in his hand.

Waiting? Stark thought suddenly. How the hell had Pollard known he was going to take a room in the hotel, let alone which room it would be?

"When you frown like that it makes you look sort of like this grizzly bear I remember seeing one time," Pollard said. Despite the lightness of his tone, the muzzle of the Colt he was pointing at Stark didn't waver even a fraction of an inch. "I imagine you're wondering what I'm doing here and how I knew where to find you."

"The questions *did* cross my mind," Stark admitted dryly.

"The answers are simple enough," Pollard said with a shrug. "I saw that eagle eye you were giving me in the saloon, and I figured you were interested in me for some reason. I asked Dinah if she knew you, and she said you were a stranger in town. That meant you had to have a place to stay if you were going to hang around and watch me, which I was convinced you planned to do. And I was right, wasn't I?"

"This is your yarn, not mine," Stark growled.

"That's right. I figured you didn't know there's a back way out of the Ace-High, a little set of outside stairs you can't see from the main room. I slipped out there, came over here, and gave Mitch downstairs a little *dinero* to make sure that you got this room if you checked in tonight." Pollard shrugged again. "The locks on these doors aren't much. It wasn't hard to come up here and get inside. Then it was just a matter of relocking the door and waiting."

"Got all of it figured out, don't you?"

"All of it except what you want with me." Pollard sat up straighter, and the noncommittal expression on his face was replaced by a look of intense scrutiny. "I don't know you, do I?"

"I don't reckon you do. My name's Earl Stark."

There was no sign of recognition in Pollard's eyes. "Why were you watching me in the saloon?"

Stark decided to try a bluff. "You've got it all wrong, mister. I never saw you before tonight, and I don't have a damn bit of interest in you

131

except for wishing you'd put that smokepole away before you get nervous and accidentally pull the trigger."

"If I pull the trigger, it won't be by accident," Pollard warned.

Stark laughed. "And if that's supposed to scare me, it ain't working."

Pollard scowled and stood up. "I've had about enough of you, Stark. You'd best give me some answers . . . now!"

Despite the Moffatt Hotel's reputation as the best such establishment in Ryanville, at least according to Doc Teague, the rooms were rather small. The bed took up most of the space in Stark's room. So when Pollard took an impatient step toward him, the movement brought him close enough for Stark to lash out with surprising speed, closing the fingers of his left hand around the barrel of Pollard's gun.

Still and all, Pollard had plenty of time to shoot, but Stark wasn't surprised when he didn't. Stark had just gambled his life on the idea that Pollard didn't want gunplay. Pollard was a stranger in town, and if the only other newcomer to Ryanville wound up dead, Pollard would be a natural suspect. He wanted to buffalo Stark into giving him some answers, but he didn't want Stark dead, not yet, anyway.

That explained why Pollard didn't pull the trigger as Stark wrenched the gun aside. But it didn't stop him from launching his other fist at Stark's face.

Stark jerked his head to the side so that Pollard's blow just grazed his jaw. He kept his left hand on the gun and bunched his right fist to drive it into Pollard's midsection. The punch slammed into Pollard's gut and doubled him over, but he was too tough for one blow to take him out of the fight. He threw himself forward, his lowered head crashing into Stark's chest and knocking the burly lawyer backward.

Feeling himself falling, Stark yanked harder on the gun and tore it from Pollard's grasp. The weapon slipped out of Stark's fingers as well and went clattering across the floor, luckily not discharging. Pollard landed on top of Stark and grappled for his throat. Stark felt the fingers close around his neck, squeezing savagely and cutting off his air.

Using his bulk, Stark heaved himself upward, throwing Pollard off to the side, but the man twisted around and managed to lash out with a booted foot, the kick catching Stark on the left shoulder. That arm went numb.

Pollard tried to kick him again, but Stark caught the man's foot in his good hand and twisted, bringing a yelp of pain from Pollard. Levering himself up with his knees, Stark threw himself forward and landed on Pollard's chest, the impact forcing the breath out of Pollard's lungs and leaving him gasping, just as Stark had been a few seconds earlier. Stark brought his right fist across in a short but powerful blow that caught Pollard in the jaw and caused his head to bounce off the planks of the floor.

That took most of the fight out of Pollard. He threw another pair of punches that Stark was able to ward off even one-handed. Stark used his weight advantage to keep Pollard pinned down and drove a knee into his belly. Another punch to the jaw sent Pollard's eyes rolling up in his head, and he slumped limply on the floor.

Stark rolled off, his chest heaving and the blood pounding in his head. He had never liked hand-to-hand fights that much, and Pollard had been a fast, dangerous opponent.

"Getting too damned old for this," Stark said as he sat up and tried to shake some of the cobwebs out of his head. He spotted Pollard's gun lying on the floor, reached over, and shoved it under the bed, where it would be out of easy reach when Pollard woke up. Then Stark knelt beside the unconscious man and patted him down for any other weapons.

He found a knife with a short but heavy blade and slid it under the bed with the Colt. A lump in the pocket of Pollard's duster proved to be a wad of money. Stark stared at the bills for a long moment, wondering if they had come from the express box on the stagecoach. Then he tossed the money on the bed and continued the search.

In addition to the roll of money, Pollard also had a wallet. Stark opened it but didn't find anything except a few more bills. There was nothing to identify Pollard, not even a scrap of paper that might have led Stark to the other members of the gang. *If* Pollard was a member of the gang.

Stark frowned and felt the wallet again. Something was strange about it, he decided. One side felt thicker than it should have. There were no secret pockets, though, at least none that he could see.

He glanced at Pollard. The man was still out cold, but he would probably be regaining consciousness soon. Stark decided to indulge his curiosity while he still had the chance.

He took out his knife and slit the leather on the wallet's thicker side, and just as he had expected, something was hidden there, some sheets of paper that had been folded up and actually sewn into the lining of the wallet. *Mighty elaborate hiding place,* Stark thought, especially for the simple hardcase that Pollard appeared to be. Appearances could damn well lie, Stark discovered a moment later when he unfolded the papers and scanned the writing on them in the lamplight.

Unless these papers were phony—and Stark had a feeling they weren't—Dan Pollard was a deputy United States marshal.

Chapter Nine

Stark was sitting on the bed, his hat, duster, and boots off and his feet propped comfortably on the coverlet, when Pollard came to a few minutes later. The LeMat was in Stark's hand, and despite his nonchalant pose, he was ready for action if Pollard proved to be difficult.

Pollard let out a groan and sat up, his hands going to his head, which was bald except for the fringe of hair around his ears. Stark grinned at him and said, "Reckon we must be what they call kindred spirits."

Pollard lifted his head and glared at Stark as he took in the sight of the big, bearded man relaxing on the bed. "What the hell do you mean by that?" he growled.

"We've both got more hair in our beards than we do on top of our heads," chuckled Stark. "We're both interested in the law, too . . . Marshal Pollard."

Breath hissed between Pollard's teeth. "I don't know what you're talking about."

Stark picked up the identification documents from the bed beside him and tossed them down to where Pollard sat on the floor. "No use denying it," Stark said. "Unless you want to tell me that you stole those bona fides, that is."

Pollard sighed. "They're mine," he admitted, wincing in pain as he moved his head. "Now what? Are you going to kill me now, or turn me over to the rest of your gang?"

"Gang?" echoed Stark, sitting up slightly. "I think you've got the wrong idea, Deputy."

"You mean to tell me you're not part of the bunch that's been hitting stagecoaches and banks all over the territory—except here in Ryanville?"

Stark's eyes narrowed. It sounded like Pollard was looking for the same men he was after. That was stretching coincidence a mite . . . but it was possible.

"You've got it all backwards, Pollard," Stark told the lawman. "You can get up off the floor and have a seat in that chair, but just like you told me a while ago, don't get ideas about trying any tricks." He gestured with the barrel of the LeMat. "I imagine you know what one of these can do at close range."

Of course, Stark wasn't going to shoot Pollard in cold blood any more than Pollard had pulled the trigger on Stark when he'd had the chance. But Pollard played along anyway, his curiosity getting the better of him as he stood up slowly and carefully and moved into the chair where he had been seated earlier.

"That's better, just a couple of gents sitting around and parleying." Stark slid the LeMat back into its holster. "There, I reckon that shows you I trust you, Pollard . . . at least part of the way."

"Who in blazes *are* you, anyway?" Pollard demanded.

"Like I told you, my name's Earl Stark. I'm no stage robber, though. I practice law over in Buffalo Flat."

Pollard's eyebrows lifted in surprise, and Stark went on, "I know, I don't look much like a lawyer. I spent a lot of years riding shotgun on stage lines from one end of Texas to the other. But I've been practicing law for about six months now. At least I was . . . until I closed up my office and started trailing the bastards who held up the stage between Buffalo Flat and Whitehorse a while back."

"I hadn't heard about that one," Pollard said with a shake of his head. "Must've happened after I was already on my way down here from headquarters. They sent me in undercover to try to get a line on the gang."

Stark nodded. "Figured as much. This bunch has been operating for a while, you say?"

"About a year." Pollard leaned forward in the chair and clasped his hands together. "They pull about two jobs a month, ranging over a four-county area. When the authorities finally started comparing notes, they marked the sites of the robberies on a map and saw that Ryanville was pretty much in the center of a big circle. Not only that, but there haven't been any holdups here in town or even in the immediate vicinity. The sheriffs of the counties involved got in touch with my boss, and when we all got together and talked

138

about it, it seemed pretty obvious that the gang could be using Ryanville as their hideout."

"And nobody in town ever noticed a bunch of hardcases moving in?" Stark's tone was skeptical.

"Nobody would if the members of the gang are living here under seemingly respectable identities."

Stark nodded slowly and rubbed his bearded jaw in thought. There might be something to what Pollard was saying, he decided. Remembering what the Kid had told him about no strangers other than Pollard being in town, he said, "They could even be folks who've lived here for a while, so the townspeople would be used to seeing them around."

"Exactly. That was one reason I couldn't figure out why you were so interested in me, because I had already decided that the members of the gang wouldn't be strangers here, and I hadn't seen you around town until tonight. But I had to find out; that's why I came over here to wait for you."

"And if I *had* been one of the gang?"

Pollard shrugged. "I reckon you'd have had to disappear. I'd've found a place to stash you until I could get you to talk and give me a line on the others." The deputy marshal gave Stark a shrewd look. "I still don't know for sure that you're not one of them. You could just be playing a mighty smooth game."

Stark shook his head and said, "I told you the truth. The girl I figured on marrying was killed in that stage holdup I mentioned. Tracking those bastards is a job to you, but it's a lot more personal to me."

"In that case, it sounds to me like the smart thing for us to do would be to work together."

Stark's eyes narrowed as he looked at the federal lawman. He still didn't completely trust Pollard, and he could tell that Pollard remained somewhat suspicious of him, too. But what he said made sense. If they were really after the same bunch of outlaws, they didn't need to be tripping over each other as they conducted their investigations.

"Wouldn't figure your boss would look kindly on your teaming up with a civilian," he pointed out.

Once again, Pollard shrugged. "When I'm out in the field like this, I make up the rules as I go along. As long as I get results, that's all that really matters."

That was sort of a high-handed attitude for a lawman to take, Stark thought, but he couldn't say much about it, considering that he was operating as a private citizen himself and not worrying about the legal aspects of the matter. He leaned over an extended a hand, saying, "I reckon we can give it a try."

Pollard gave him a firm handshake. "Just don't get in my way, Stark."

"And don't you get in *mine*," Stark warned, equally grim. "Now, tell me—what's that saloon girl got to do with all this?"

For the first time, Pollard grinned. "You mean

Dinah? Hell, who knows more about what goes on in town than a gal like that? She hears all the gossip about the respectable folks and the not-so-respectable alike."

"So you've been trying to get information out of her while you're romancing her?"

"That's right," nodded Pollard. "And it's been one of the more pleasant parts of the job, too, even if it hasn't been very productive so far."

It seemed to Stark that Pollard was just using his assignment as an excuse to do some romping with a pretty girl, but that was Pollard's business, not his. And it was probably true that Dinah would be privy to quite a bit of information about the goings-on in Ryanville. Men had a habit of talking to women like that once they'd finished their dallying, and under those circumstances a gent's tongue got looser than he might have intended it to.

"What *have* you found out?" Stark asked.

"That there haven't been any strangers in Ryanville lately—except for you."

Stark resisted the impulse to snort in disgust. He'd found out that much less than five minutes after he'd ridden into town, only Pollard had been pointed out as the other stranger in Ryanville. But he saw no point in antagonizing the man if they were going to try to work together.

"Well, we've established that if the gang is here, they're lying low and pretending to be honest citizens," Stark said dryly. "What do we do next?"

"Maybe we should try to find out if anybody's been taking any trips out of town," suggested Pollard.

Stark considered the idea and nodded slowly. If their theory was correct, the bandits would have to ride out on a regular basis. Maybe the Kid would have some information that could help them on that score. The friendly young man was in a good position to observe the comings and goings of Ryanville's citizens.

Stark leaned over again and fished Pollard's gun and knife from under the bed. He held out the weapons to the deputy and commented, "Reckon we've got to trust each other. Here."

Pollard stood up, took the weapons, holstered the Colt, and slid the knife back in its sheath. He asked, "How do you want to do this?"

"Let's get together first thing in the morning. I know somebody we can ask about any unusual trips made by these townies."

"All right." Pollard fixed Stark with an intense gaze. "You'd better be playing straight with me. I'll be watching my back."

"You and me both, pard," Stark said coolly.

Pollard settled his hat on his head and winced as it touched some of the goose eggs raised during the fight. He went to the door, threw one more narrow-eyed glance over his shoulder, and left the room.

Stark leaned back against the headboard of the bed. He didn't really trust Pollard, didn't particularly like the man, but the deputy marshal seemed competent enough. With any luck, they'd track down the outlaw gang, and they didn't have to like each other to do that. Once they'd located the bandits, Pollard could arrest any of them who survived capture. That would make things all nice and legal-like, and Stark wouldn't have to feel so much like a vigilante. Under the circumstances, it was almost as if he was an unofficial deputy himself.

Pollard could take the credit, though; Stark wasn't interested in that. All he wanted was to see the murderous bastards who'd killed Laura brought to justice.

Chapter Ten

Stark had a good breakfast the next morning at the Red Top, enjoying the thick slices of ham, the hot, fluffy biscuits, and the mountain of hash browns the waitress brought to him. She left the whole pot of coffee at his table, and he washed down the food with several cups of the strong black brew. Before he finished, Dan Pollard came into the café and headed for his table.

"Thought I might find you here," the lawman said. "Is all that food for you, or are you expecting a troop of cavalry to join you?"

Stark ignored the sarcastic comment and jerked a thumb at the vacant chair across from him. "Sit down. No point in trying to keep it a secret that we know each other."

"Well, we're both strangers in town," Pollard said as he pulled back the chair, dropped his hat on the table, and sat down. "Natural enough that we'd get together, I suppose."

Stark nodded and kept eating. When the waitress noticed Pollard, she came over and took his order. While he was waiting for flapjacks and bacon, he said, "It's too early to talk to Dinah. She won't be awake until noon, at least. What do you think we should do in the meantime?"

"I've got an idea or two," replied Stark, not

mentioning the Kid. The café was fairly busy this morning, and with nearly everybody in town under suspicion to some degree, it probably wouldn't be wise to talk about their plans. Evidently Pollard agreed, because he nodded and was silent as he nursed his coffee.

Stark finished his food just about the time the waitress brought Pollard's, but he didn't mind sitting and ruminating for a bit while the deputy ate. When Pollard was through, they left enough money on the table to cover their bills, then strolled out into the morning sunshine.

It was a pretty day here in the foothills, the sun shining brightly and a few puffs of white cloud in the blue sky overhead. As Stark and Pollard paused on the boardwalk in front of the Red Top, Stark's attention was drawn to an enclosed wagon parked nearby. The words *Phineas Langley, Photographist Extraordinaire* were painted on the sideboards in big, garish red letters. A man in a frock coat and top hat was trying the reins of the wagon's mules to the hitchrack in front of the boardwalk. That would be Phineas Langley, Stark decided. The man was tall and slender and had a small goatee that gave a rather devilish cast to his lean face.

Pollard nudged Stark with an elbow, then asked with a grin, "Want to get your picture made?"

Stark shook his head. "I reckon we've got better things to do than waste our money on some itinerant photographist. Come on."

He stepped off the boardwalk and strode down the street toward the livery stable, Pollard falling in beside him. If anyone in the street or strolling along the boardwalks paid any undue attention to them, neither man noticed it.

As Stark had hoped, the Kid was at the livery stable, forking down hay from the loft. Stark called up to him as they entered the barn, "Howdy, Kid. How's that Appaloosa of mine?"

The Kid paused in his work, leaning on his pitchfork to look down at Stark and Pollard. "Mornin', Mr. Stark," he said with a grin. "Your horse is just fine. You can look in on him if you'd like."

"I'll do that," Stark said. He spotted the Appaloosa in one of the stalls and walked over to the horse to pat it on the flank. The Appaloosa seemed content enough, although it got a little frisky at the sight of Stark. Probably wanted to get out and run awhile to stretch its legs, Stark thought. Maybe—if the Kid had the right answers to some questions—Stark would get to oblige the old boy before the day was over.

The Kid climbed down the ladder from the loft with the agility of youth and walked over to the stall. He was frowning a little as he inclined his head toward Pollard, who was waiting just inside the barn doors. "I see you met the stranger," the Kid said in a low voice to Stark.

"Yep, he was just the man I was looking for." Stark rubbed the Appaloosa's nose. "Listen, Kid, I've got another question for you."

146

Evidently satisfied that Pollard was all right, the Kid grinned and said, "Shoot."

"Have you noticed anybody—not strangers, but people who live in Ryanville—taking any trips lately? Riding out for, say, four or five days or even a week?"

The frown reappeared on the Kid's face. "That's a mighty funny question, Mr. Stark. You mind if I ask why you want to know?"

"Personal business," Stark said curtly.

The Kid hesitated, as if unsure whether or not to be offended by Stark's attitude. Then he shrugged and said, "Doesn't really matter. I haven't seen anybody doing anything like that. The cowboys who work on the spreads north of here come and go, of course, but most other folks stay close to home. No place around here to go to, I suppose."

Stark turned over the information in his head. It was possible the outlaws worked as cowhands, but riding jobs tended to tie a man down and make it hard to get away without being noticed. Still, it might be worthwhile to ride out to some of the closer spreads and inquire among the owners if any of their hands had been missing from time to time.

"Thanks," he said to the Kid. "How about saddling up this old boy for me? My friend and I are going to take a ride." Stark turned to the lawman. "Where are you keeping your horse, Pollard?"

"Right here," replied Pollard. He asked the

Kid, "You remember my horse, don't you, son? That chestnut mare?"

The Kid nodded. "Sure, I'll saddle up both of them for you gents. Take me just a few minutes."

Stark walked outside the barn again, and Pollard joined him. "You and that boy seem pretty friendly," Pollard commented. "I just turned my horse over to him and went on about my business."

"He's the eager sort, wants to help," Stark said. "I figured it might be handy to get him on my side." The big man chuckled. "Calls himself the Kid and reads dime novels about desperadoes."

"I've seen a hundred like him," Pollard said with a shake of his head. "He's probably got some old pistol stashed away somewhere that he uses to practice a fast draw."

"Wouldn't doubt it a bit," agreed Stark.

A few minutes later, the Kid brought the two horses, Stark's Appaloosa and Pollard's chestnut, out of the barn, saddled and ready to ride. Stark noted that his greener and the Winchester were packed in the saddle boot, just as he had left them. He thanked the Kid and swung up onto the Appaloosa.

"Where are we going?" Pollard asked as they rode out of town, heading north on one of the cross streets that became a trail as the houses of Ryanville were left behind.

"There are several ranches north of here," explained Stark. "The Kid said nobody came and went from town recently, other than the cowboys who work on those spreads."

Pollard frowned a little. "You think those bandits could be working as cowhands? Doesn't seem very likely to me."

"You've been around here longer than I have," Stark said. "Got any better ideas?"

Pollard grimaced and shook his head. "Not really. I guess we might as well poke around a little."

"That's what I thought."

The two men spent the morning riding through the foothills, following the winding trail. Stark could tell from the ruts that wagons used this path from time to time, ranch wagons coming into town for supplies, most likely. That trade would be the real lifeblood of Ryanville, because without the ranches there would be no compelling reason for the town's existence.

The trail forked, and they took the left-hand turn, moving a little deeper into the hills. After another half-mile, they could see a cluster of log buildings against the face of a steep hill. Stark and Pollard rode up to the largest of the buildings, and Stark called out, "Hello, the house! Anybody home?"

"Over here!"

The voice came from their right, and they turned in their saddles to see a gray-haired, bowlegged old man walking toward them from one of the other buildings. Smoke rose from the building's chimney, and Stark figured it was the cookshack. He pegged the old man, who wore an apron, as the ranch cook.

"Howdy," Stark said to the man with a friendly nod. "Where is everybody?"

The old man snorted. "Where'n hell do you think they'd be in the middle of the day like this? The foreman and the hands're all out workin', where they're supposed to be."

"What spread is this?" asked Pollard.

"Forked Tail. What business is it of your'n?"

"We're looking for the boss," Stark said. "Thought maybe you'd have a couple of riding jobs open."

The cook glared at Stark. "Pity the hoss that'd have to carry you around the range all day, old son. Anyway, they ain't no jobs. Our crew's full up."

"Nobody rode off lately, lit out without giving notice?"

"Huh! If they did, they wouldn't last long. Reese'd run 'em off, sure as hell."

"Who's Reese?"

"Foreman and ranch manager. Runs the place for the syndicate back East that owns it."

Stark nodded. "Well, we'll be riding on, then. Thanks anyway."

"Hold on, hold on," the old cook said quickly. "Just 'cause we ain't hirin' right now don't mean you boys got to run off. Light and set a spell. The hands'll be comin' in for noon grub 'fore long, and you're welcome to join 'em. Ain't nobody can say the Forked Tail ain't hospitable."

150

"That's all right, old-timer," Stark said. "Anybody asks us, we'll say the Forked Tail is a downright hospitable place. But we've got to be riding anyway."

"All right, then, go on with you. Welcome to stop back by anytime you're in the neighborhood, though."

Stark lifted a hand in farewell. "We'll remember that."

He and Pollard rode away, heading back toward the main trail. When they were out of earshot of the ranch, Pollard asked, "You reckon that old coot was telling the truth?"

Stark nodded slowly. "I imagine so. He was a mite testy, but he struck me as the type who liked to talk. If that foreman is as tough as he said, any of the hands who took off to go rob stagecoaches and banks would've been fired, and the old man would have told us about it. I reckon we can cross off the Forked Tail as a likely hideout for the gang."

An hour later they reached the next ranch, the Diamond J. Some of the crew were there for lunch, and this time Stark and Pollard joined them. The foreman told them that no riding jobs were available at the moment.

"Wrong time of the year for that, boys," the man said. "Come back around spring roundup, and I reckon I might have something then."

"We'll sure do that, Mr. Breen," Stark told him. "This must be a good spread to work for, since you don't seem to have any trouble keeping hands."

"All my men have been with me for a while," agreed Breen. "But I always have to hire a few extra men at roundup time."

When they were riding away again, Pollard asked, "What do you think?"

"I think we're on a wild-goose chase, Dan, but I don't see anything else to do except play out the hand."

"Could be our thinking's all wrong," Pollard said slowly, deep in thought. "What if the gang doesn't have any connection with Ryanville at all?"

"Then we move on to Cross Cut or one of the other settlements around here and start looking all over again," Stark answered without hesitation. "It could be just coincidence that Ryanville hasn't been hit, but I know one thing—I'm not giving up."

"Like you said, it's personal with you and a job with me . . . but I'm not much of a mind to give up, either."

Stark grinned at the deputy marshal, his liking for Pollard becoming a little stronger. Given time, he supposed Pollard could grow on a person.

During the afternoon they visited two more ranches, with the same results as their stops at the Forked Tail and the Diamond J. All the hands in the area seemed to be honest cowboys, not above blowing off steam and causing a ruckus in town on payday but not the sort who'd go around robbing and killing. Late in the afternoon, Stark and Pollard turned their horses toward Ryanville, knowing it would be after nightfall by the time they got back to town but confident they could follow the trail in the dark.

"What next?" mused Pollard as they rode along, the sun almost touching the craggy tops of the mountains to the west.

"Reckon you can try again to get some information out of that Dinah gal," replied Stark, "and I'll talk to the Kid again in the morning. Maybe he's thought of something else that he forgot today."

"I wouldn't put too much faith in anything a wide-eyed youngster tells you," Pollard warned.

Stark shook his head. "I'd say the Kid's as reliable a source as some saloon girl."

"Well, I reckon we'll see," Pollard said.

Stark kept the Appaloosa trotting along smartly. Despite what the cook at the Forked Tail had said, the horse had carried Stark all day without seeming to get too tired. In that strange manner of communication between horse and rider that sometimes existed if a man was lucky in his choice of mount, Stark knew that the Appaloosa had in fact enjoyed the day.

The sun was almost behind the mountains, leaving a garish red glow in the sky and gathering shadows on the ground, when Stark felt the sudden tug on his duster, as if an unseen hand had reached out from nowhere and yanked on the long coat. He recognized it for what it was, and even as he opened his mouth to yell "Ambush!" he heard the distant crack of a rifle.

Stark tumbled out of the saddle, sliding the Winchester from its sheath as he went. He slapped the Appaloosa on the rump as he sprawled in the dust of the trail. The horse leapt ahead, and Stark hoped that would take it out of the line of fire. He came up on his hands and knees and then scrambled to his feet, heading toward a clump of rocks at the side of the path.

As he ran, he heard a sharp whinny from Pollard's horse, along with the deputy's surprised cursing. Stark threw himself down among the rocks. A bullet whined off one of them as the bushwhacker's rifle spoke again. Stark twisted his head and saw Pollard struggling with the chestnut. The horse was trying to bolt, and one of Pollard's boots appeared to be caught in the stirrup.

If the chestnut broke into a gallop, Pollard would be dragged along behind it and beaten into a bloody mess by the rough trail. But that wasn't the only danger. The bushwhacker could switch targets at any time and try to hit Pollard, although it would be hard the way the lawman was hopping around and dancing with the spooked horse.

Finally Pollard got his boot loose and threw himself toward the side of the trail. His black hat flew off his head as the bushwhacker fired again, and the silver conchos around the band sparkled in the fading light as the hat spun through the air. Pollard landed hard on his belly at the edge of the trail, the air knocked out of his lungs with a *whoof!*

"Pollard!" called Stark. "You hit?"

By way of answer, Pollard crawled quickly into some brush, moving faster than he would have been able to if a bullet had found him. He shouted back, "Keep your own head down, damn it!"

Stark intended to do just that. The ambusher fired a couple of more times, one of the bullets ricocheting off the rocks again, the other ripping through the thicket where Pollard was concealed. Both shots missed their true targets, though.

The bushwhacker had picked a hell of a poor time for an ambush, Stark thought, and that was lucky for him and Pollard. The light was bad and getting worse by the minute. Still, the bastard had been able to see well enough to know where they had gone to ground, and he could keep peppering the rocks and the brush with slugs and hope a stray shot would do the job. With enough lead flying around, anything was possible.

It was time to do a little fighting back. Hoping he wouldn't come eyeball-to-eyeball with a bullet, Stark edged his head up and spotted the muzzle flash as the bushwhacker fired again at the thicket where Pollard was holed up. The son of a bitch was on a hillside to the west, about a hundred yards away. Before the ambusher could change his aim and fire at the rocks again, Stark opened up on the spot where he had seen the orange-red flash, firing the Winchester as fast as he could work the lever and jack fresh cartridges into the chamber. Over the rolling thunder of the rifle blasts, he shouted to Pollard, "Get out of there!"

Pollard seized the chance to secure some better cover. Like a rapidly moving shadow in the gathering dusk, he darted out of the brush, ran about ten yards, and threw himself into a small, narrow gully deep enough to protect him. When Stark saw the lawman vanish into the gully, he pulled back the Winchester and hunkered down in the rocks as best he could, knowing that he was going to get some return fire.

Sure enough, the bushwhacker opened up again. Pollard didn't have a long gun to take the heat off Stark, so for minutes that seemed like hours, Stark had to lie there amid the rocks, listening to the vicious whine and snarl of rifle rounds bouncing off the stones. Sparks kicked up by the shots danced around him. Stark kept his head down and did some plain and fancy cussing, unsure whether he was saying the words out loud or not.

Then, abruptly, the fusillade ended, and the silence left in its wake was rather disconcerting by contrast. Stark didn't move except to turn his head slightly. In the slice of sky he could see from his awkward position, the last glow of sunset was fading to black, and the stars were beginning to appear. The moon wouldn't be up for a while, and in a matter of moments it would be dark enough for him and Pollard to risk leaving their cover and catching their horses.

A distant clatter of hoofbeats reached Stark's ears. Pollard must have heard it, too, because he called out, "He's leaving!"

"Hold on," Stark urged. "Could be just a trick to try to draw us out." That was unlikely given the lack of light, but Stark knew that moving too fast could get a man killed.

The hoofbeats faded, and Stark and Pollard waited a good ten minutes after utter silence had fallen again.

Finally Stark said, "Reckon he's gone, all right." He stood up slowly, ready to fling himself back behind the rocks if anybody took a shot at him.

No one did. Pollard emerged from the gully and brushed his pants off as he walked over to join Stark. "That was too damned close," the deputy said fervently.

"Amen," Stark agreed. He stepped onto the trail and picked up Pollard's hat, slipping a finger through the bullet hole in its crown. "You almost got that skull of yours ventilated," he said as he handed the hat to Pollard.

"And he might've got me in that brush if you hadn't given me a chance to find a better place to fort up." Pollard shook his head in disgust at the hat and put it on. "Thanks, Big Earl."

Stark looked sharply at him. "How'd you know that's what they used to call me?"

"I heard the stories about a fella named Stark who rode shotgun on the stage lines hereabouts.

I'm surprised there's not any dime novels about you, like there are about old Deadwood Dick."

"I can do without that," declared Stark. Since Pollard had figured out who he was, he went on, "I'm the one they called Big Earl, all right, but I'm not riding shotgun anymore. Gave it up a while back and started practicing law instead."

"Yeah, you said that. It threw me a little for a while. But then when I saw how you reacted to that ambush, I knew you had to be Big Earl."

Stark gestured down the trail toward Ryanville. "Let's see if we can catch up to our horses." As they started walking, he continued, "What do you think about that ambush?"

"Whoever was waiting for us picked the wrong time of day," Pollard said. "There was enough light for some good shots at us, but once he missed, he couldn't keep us pinned down for the long haul until he got us."

"Maybe now was the only chance he had," mused Stark. "There's something else that bothers me even more."

"What's that?"

"Why bushwhack us at all?"

Pollard stopped and looked over at Stark in the starlight. "That's a damned good question. We're both strangers around here, and there shouldn't be anybody with too big a grudge against us. I've had a few deliberate run-ins with folks in town, but nothing to prompt a bushwhacking."

"That rifleman had another reason, then, and

the only one I can figure is that we've been asking questions. Could be somebody didn't like us getting too nosy."

"Then that could mean—"

"We're closer to that gang than we thought," Stark finished.

It was the only explanation that made sense, Stark thought as they caught sight of the Appaloosa and Pollard's chestnut, both animals casually cropping grass at the side of the trail. Stark hadn't expected the Appaloosa to stray far, and luckily Pollard's mount had stopped when the other horse did. Talking gently to the horses, the men approached slowly and took hold of the dangling reins, then mounted up and started down the trail toward town. Stark didn't expect any more ambush attempts, and he turned out to be right. No one bothered them, and an hour later the lights of Ryanville came into view.

"What do we do now?" Pollard asked before they parted company for the night.

"We do the only thing we can," Stark said. "We keep poking the hornet's nest until we see what flies out."

Chapter Eleven

A knock sounded on the door of Stark's hotel room the next morning before he had left for breakfast. He was buckling on his shell belt at the time, so he put his hand on the butt of the LeMat and went over to the door.

Standing to one side, he gave a noncommittal grunt, knowing it was difficult to pinpoint the exact location of such a sound. Anyone firing a gun through the door would probably miss.

A moment later, a familiar but puzzled voice asked through the panel, "Mr. Stark? You in there?"

Stark relaxed a little and reached for the knob with his free hand. He swung the door open and said, "What are you doing here, Kid? Nothing wrong down at the stable, is there?"

"No, sir." The Kid stepped into the room, his hat in his hands. "Something did happen, though, and I thought you might want to know about it."

"What's that?"

"Doc Teague and that old fella who works for him—the one they call Pops—they both rode out of town this morning."

Stark frowned and shook his head. "Together?"

"Nope. Pops left first, but it wasn't half an hour before Doc came down to the stable and got his saddle horse, too. He headed west out of town, same direction as Pop went."

Stark didn't see anything unusual about what the Kid was telling him. It would have been a little strange if Doc and Pops had left town together, what with Doc owning the saloon and Pops merely working there as the swamper, but there could have been any number of reasons for them to ride out of Ryanville separately.

Stark began, "I appreciate you coming down here to tell me about this, Kid, but—"

"They were both wearing dusters," the Kid said.

Stark's frown deepened. That put things in a different light, enough to get all of his attention.

"You see," the Kid hurried on, "I could tell that you and Mr. Pollard were a mite upset about something last evening when you brought your horses back, and I thought all night about what you asked me yesterday morning. You know, about folks from here in Ryanville leaving every now and then for a while. Something was bothering me and I kept trying to remember what it was, and then this morning when Mr. Teague and Pops rode out, I remembered."

"And?" Stark prodded.

"Well . . . I don't want to get Mr. Teague in trouble, since he's a good customer and all—him and Miss Belle have a surrey they keep at the stable and take out for rides in the country—but

161

anyway, I remembered that this isn't the first time Mr. Teague and Pops have left town like this. Once Mr. Teague had some other gents with him, too, fellas I didn't know and hadn't ever seen before. I think . . . I'm not sure, but I'd swear those other men were wearing dusters, too."

Stark felt like grabbing the Kid by the shoulders and shaking him, demanding why he hadn't been able to remember all this before now. From the sound of it, Doc Teague and Pops might well be members of the gang Stark and Pollard were after, and now they had already left town, maybe riding out to rob and murder someplace else.

Reining in his temper and impatience, Stark asked, "Are you sure about all this, Kid?"

The Kid's head bobbed up and down. "Yes, sir, Mr. Stark. Certain sure. I saw 'em."

"And they took the trail west, into the mountains?"

"That's right."

"What sort of horses were they riding?"

"Mr. Teague was on a big bay gelding, and Pops rides a grulla mustang."

"Thanks, Kid." Stark reached for his hat and coat. "You'd better be getting on back to the stable."

"Mr. Stark?" The Kid lifted a hand to stop him, then hesitated.

"What is it?" growled Stark as he shrugged into his duster, anxious to collect Pollard and get started on the trail of Doc and Pops.

"I've tried not to pry, but I know you and Mr. Pollard are after somebody. Looks like Mr. Teague and Pops might be tied up in whatever brought you here to Ryanville. I . . . I'd like to ride with you and help you if I can."

Stark had been afraid the youngster was going to make that offer. He shook his head and said firmly, "You've done enough, Kid. You've been a big help already, just by coming here this morning and telling me what you saw and what you remembered. You head on back to the stable now."

"But—"

"Go on," Stark said, his tone not allowing any argument. "You can saddle the horses for me and Pollard when you get there."

The Kid sighed and said reluctantly, "Well, all right." He settled his hat on his head. "But if you need any more help, you just let me know."

"We'll do that, Kid," Stark assured him, not meaning a word of it.

He and Pollard would handle this. With any luck, before the day was over they'd be one step closer to bringing the gang of thieves and killers to justice.

As soon as the Kid was gone, Stark hurried down the corridor to Pollard's room. The lawman had given Stark his room number the night before when they returned to Ryanville. Stark rapped sharply on the door, calling softly, "Pollard? It's me, Stark." He figured the deputy would be just as cautious answering an unknown knock at the door as he was.

The door swung open. Pollard stood there with the Colt in his hand, ready for instant use. When he saw that Stark was alone, he took his thumb off the hammer and holstered the revolver. "What's up?" he asked.

"The Kid just told me that Doc Teague and Pops, the swamper from the Ace-High, rode out of town this morning."

Pollard looked blank. "So?"

"They didn't ride out together, but they left only a little while apart, and they went in the same direction. *And* they were wearing dusters."

With a dubious look, Pollard said, "You don't think—"

"I think it's worth following them and taking a look-see for ourselves. When they left town it jogged the Kid's memory, and he says this isn't the first time they've both been gone at the same time. Once before Teague had other men with him, too."

"Other members of that gang?"

"Could be."

Pollard shook his head. "I'm not convinced. Teague's a successful businessman. Why would he need to be a desperado?"

"Did you ever ask yourself how he got so successful?" Stark pointed out. "He's in a perfect position to be ramrodding that gang. His wife can run the saloon while he's out pulling jobs with the gang, and nobody would ever think to question where he got his money when he turned up with his share of the loot. They'd just think the saloon was even more profitable than it really is."

Pollard rubbed his jaw in thought. "There could be something to what you say," he admitted after a moment.

"I'm damned sure there's something to it," Stark insisted, all of his instincts telling him that he was right. "If we get moving now, we can pick up their trail. They're probably going to rendezvous with the rest of the gang and pull another job. We can stop them before they kill anybody else."

Pollard nodded abruptly. "All right, you've convinced me. Let's ride."

They stopped at the Red Top for biscuits and sausage to eat while they were traveling. The Kid had the Appaloosa and the chestnut saddled and ready to go when they reached the livery stable.

"I still wish I was going along with you," the Kid said wistfully as Stark and Pollard swung up into their saddles.

"Maybe another time, Kid."

The youngster looked up at them. "You're riding into trouble, aren't you?"

For a second, Stark didn't answer. Then he decided that the Kid deserved a response. After all, without the information he had given them, the two men wouldn't be setting out on the trail of Doc Teague and Pops. "Maybe," Stark said with a nod. "If we're lucky."

The terrain gradually grew more and more rugged as Stark and Pollard followed the trail through the foothills, which extended several miles out from the main range of mountains. This route led to the settlement known as Cross Cut, but Stark had a feeling that wasn't where Doc and Pops were heading. They probably had a place up here in the mountains where they could meet with others to plan their jobs. Stark hoped he and Pollard could catch the whole gang in one fell swoop.

Stark kept his eyes on the left side of the trail while Pollard watched the right, both men looking for tracks. As a shotgun guard, Stark hadn't been required to do a great deal of tracking, but he was keen eyed except when it came to paperwork, and he was sure he could spot the telltale signs of riders moving off the trail.

By midmorning neither man had seen any sign, and Pollard was beginning to get discouraged. "How far do you reckon they went?" he asked as they reined in to rest the horses for a spell.

"No way of knowing." Stark looked around. The trail followed a small stream that wound through the heights of the timber-covered hills all around them. The creek sparkled in the sunlight, and the air was warm and full of the smell of wildflowers. It would have been a mighty pretty day, Stark thought, if he and his companion had not been on the trail of a gang of killers.

After a couple of minutes, Stark heeled the Appaloosa into motion again. Pollard rode beside him. Both men switched their gaze from the trail to the hills around them, watching for any flash of sunlight on gunmetal that might warn of another ambush attempt. They seemed to be alone in the hills, however. There were plenty of birds, deer, raccoons, and squirrels around here, but no people, outlaws or otherwise.

Stark was somewhat discouraged, too, although he kept hoping they would find what they were looking for. It was possible that Doc and Pops had given them the slip, left the trail in one of the rocky stretches where tracks would be hard to spot. Hell, it was possible the two men had nothing to do with the stage robberies. But after a few more minutes of riding, he and Pollard rounded a bend and reined in sharply at the sight of a building up ahead beside the trail.

"Into the trees," hissed Stark, turning the Appaloosa toward a thick growth of aspen to the right along the creek. He and Pollard rode into the cover of the trees and dismounted to take a better look at the shack, where five horses were tied up.

"Looks like it might have been a roadhouse at one time," Pollard commented in a quiet voice as he studied the building made of crude planks.

Stark nodded his agreement, thinking of Kilroy's place over in the Maricopas, where he had gotten the first clue leading him to Ryanville. There was an air of general disrepair about this building, though, leading him to believe it had been abandoned sometime in the past.

Of course, an abandoned roadhouse would make a good meeting place for the gang he and Pollard were seeking. Stark's eyes narrowed as he looked at the horses tied in front of the shack. Two of them were a bay and a grulla, the horses Doc and Pops were riding when they left Ryanville, according to the Kid.

"That's them," Stark said. "I'm sure of it."

"Then we'd best slip up on that building and see if we can find out what's going on inside."

Stark agreed, though his heart was thudding heavily as he and Pollard moved quietly out of the aspens and started cat-footing toward the abandoned roadhouse. Up ahead, within a hundred yards, were the men responsible for Laura's death. A part of him wanted to kick in the door and go in with the LeMat roaring. Even though he liked both Doc and Pops, he wanted to see them die, just as Laura had. He wanted vengeance.

He gritted his teeth. He was a law-abiding man, he warned himself. More than that, he was an attorney, sworn to uphold the law. No matter how much his soul cried out for revenge, he couldn't allow himself to turn vigilante. He had to give the outlaws a chance to surrender.

And if they chose not to . . . well, then, the lead could fly and devil take the hindmost.

168

Pollard motioned silently with his free hand—he had already drawn his Colt with the other—and he and Stark split up, veering toward either side of the door, which sagged on ancient leather hinges. There were no windows in the cabin, but as they leaned against the walls, they could hear the murmur of voices coming from inside. Stark slipped the LeMat from its holster and held it close beside him, his thumb on the hammer in readiness.

Suddenly, as he glanced at Pollard, he saw a flicker of motion behind the lawman as someone stepped around the corner of the shack. Stark was about to cry out a warning when he saw Pollard's eyes widen and knew that the jaws of the trap were about to close on *him*, too. A faint crunching of gravel came from behind him, and someone pressed the cold mouth of a gun muzzle against the back of his neck.

"Don't move, Mr. Stark," said a totally unexpected voice, "or I'll be forced to shoot you."

"You be still, too, Dan," ordered the person who had gotten the drop on the deputy marshal. "I'd hate to have to blow your head off."

A delicate hand with slender fingers and long red nails reached up and plucked the LeMat out of Stark's grasp. He said incredulously, "Miss Belle?"

Belle Teague pressed the gun barrel harder against Stark's neck. "Get Mr. Pollard's gun, Dinah."

The pretty saloon girl reached around from behind Pollard and took his Colt.

Pollard stood stiffly, his eyes wide with amazement. "Dinah?" he said. "You're part of this?"

"Of course," Dinah said. "We both are."

Belle lifted her voice and called, "You and the others can come out now, Doc. Dinah and I have these two."

The door of the cabin opened, and Doc Teague stepped out, managing to make even the long duster and the trail clothes under it look somewhat elegant. He was followed by Pops, who wore a pleased smile on his lined, weathered features.

"Well, that trap sprung just the way it was supposed to," Doc said with great satisfaction. "They walked right into it. Now maybe we can find out what they're really after, just like—"

Another duster-wearing figure nudged his horse out of the trees behind Stark and Pollard, looking just as pleased with himself as the other members of the gang as he said, "Just like I planned."

It was the Kid.

Chapter Twelve

Well, if this wasn't a hell of a mess, Stark thought, then he had never seen one.

He and Pollard were sitting on rickety ladder-back chairs inside the building—an abandoned roadhouse, just as Stark had thought. A small bar still sat in one corner of the room, and tin whiskey signs were tacked to the planks of the wall behind them. Stark and Pollard weren't tied up, but Doc and Pops stood flanking them, six-guns in hand, ready if either of the two prisoners tried anything funny.

Belle and Dinah had put their guns away. They were dressed considerably differently from the last time Stark had seen them. Now they were wearing denim pants and men's shirts beneath their jackets.

The Kid stood in front of the chairs in which Stark and Pollard sat. His duster was pushed back, and he had one hand on the butt of the pistol he wore, while the thumb of the other hand was hooked casually behind the shell belt. Stark figured it was a pose; the boy was trying to look like one of the desperadoes from his dime novels—which was exactly what he was, of course.

Because one thing had become obvious in the

short time that Stark and Pollard had been captives of the outlaw gang: despite his youth and innocent appearance, the Kid was the master-mind behind the whole thing.

"Might as well talk," the Kid told them. "You two aren't going anywhere until you tell me who you are and what you're really after in Ryanville."

"We've already told you," Pollard began wearily. "This is all just a misunderstanding—"

Stark had had enough, and it was obvious the Kid wasn't going to accept just any lie. He interrupted Pollard by saying, "Damn it, you might as well quit trying to sell him that yarn. He ain't buying."

"None of us are," Doc warned. "We could just shoot the both of you and have done with it."

The Kid lifted his hands. "Hold on, hold on. No need for anybody to lose his temper. You're going to be reasonable now, aren't you, Mr. Stark?"

"We were looking for you," Stark said bluntly. "You already figured that out. No point in denying it."

"Well, that's true," the Kid grinned, evidently pleased at the indirect compliment Stark had paid him. "But do you know who we are?"

Stark took a deep breath. "You're the gang that's been holding up banks and stagecoaches all over this part of the country . . . except Ryanville."

Pops groused, "I told you that'd lead some-body to us, Kid. I told you."

"Nobody's found us in a year except these two," the Kid shot back. "And we can deal with them." He faced Stark and Pollard again. "What do you want with us?"

"Why, to join up, of course," Stark replied without hesitation.

The Kid's eyebrows lifted a little in surprise. Then he said, "Keep talking."

Stark glanced over at Pollard, hoping the lawman would play along. "I've been on the dodge for a while, ever since things got a mite too hot for me down along the Rio. Been looking to throw in with a bunch like yours, and a while back I got to talking with a fella at a robbers' roost over in the Maricopas. Said his name was Lee Roy and that he rode sometimes with a gang that operated out of Ryanville."

Doc bit out a curse. "I told you Lee Roy's mouth would get us in trouble, Kid. He was always too fond of talking when he'd had too much to drink."

The Kid waved off Doc's complaint and said to Stark, "What happened to Lee Roy? We haven't seen him around in a while."

"Some hombre came in and shot him while we were talking. He never did say what his argu-ment was with Lee Roy, and I didn't have a chance to ask him. He was shooting in my general direction, so I shot back."

"Killed him, did you?"

"Seemed to be the thing to do at the time," Stark said.

"Well, that explains why Lee Roy never came back," mused the Kid. "So you rode over here looking for us after that. What about Pollard?"

"Figured he might be one of the gang," Stark replied easily. "You heard the questions I asked you, Kid. I was looking for hardcase strangers." He glanced at the figures surrounding him and Pollard. "Not a bunch of respectable citizens like you folks. Got to admit, it's a smooth operation you've got set up."

"Thanks," the Kid said. "I came up with the idea and brought in Doc and Pops. Belle and Dinah sort of came along for the ride, and it's been a good one."

"You've got women riding with you on your holdups?" Pollard sounded as if he couldn't comprehend the idea.

"Dinah's gone along with us a time or two," Doc said. "Belle handles the Ace-High while I'm gone."

Stark had figured as much, but under the circumstances he wasn't too happy about having his theory confirmed.

The Kid added, "We use some other gents from time to time, too, like Lee Roy, whenever a job calls for more help. Generally we pay 'em off and they move on, though."

Stark nodded. "Sounds like Pollard and me would fit right in. Why don't you boys put those guns up so we can all talk reasonable-like?"

"Not just yet." The Kid turned to Pollard. "How about you? What's your story?"

"About the same as Stark's," Pollard said with a shrug. "I figured you had a hideout somewhere in or around Ryanville, and I came to these parts hoping to hook up with you. Once Stark and I compared notes, it seemed easier to look for you together."

Stark managed to chuckle. "I could see Doc and Pops being mixed up with an outlaw gang, but I never figured you to be running things, Kid. In case you don't know it, that's a compliment."

With a laugh that was half-sneer, the Kid said, "Those stupid bastards back in town have never suspected me of a thing. They don't know they've got a genius among them."

Calling himself a genius might be stretching things, Stark thought, but the Kid was right on one count: No one in town ever would have suspected his true nature. He had fooled Stark completely, and Stark liked to think he was a pretty good judge of character. He might have to adjust his thinking . . . if he survived this mess.

Pops spoke up for the first time since Stark and Pollard had been brought into the shack. "I don't know if I believe anything they're sayin'," he declared. "We could just shoot 'em like Doc said and not worry about it."

"You and your brother are too bloodthirsty," the Kid said. "We might be able to use these two."

Stark glanced from Doc to Pops and back

again. The revelation that they were brothers came as a surprise, but now that he studied them, he could see the resemblance. Pops was quite a bit older, but they definitely favored each other. Stark just hoped they wouldn't be able to persuade the Kid to go along with what they wanted.

Belle said, "I don't think there's any need to shoot them, Kid. At least not yet. They could be telling the truth."

Dinah leaned closer to Pollard and ran her fingertips along his bearded jaw. "Yeah, let's let them live, Kid, for a while anyway. I sort of like this one."

Stiffly, Pollard said, "All the time I was trying to get information out of you, you were just laughing at me, weren't you?"

"Not all the time," Dinah said huskily. "Most of it, maybe, but not all the time."

Stark was about to suggest that they get on with it, whatever their decision, when the creaking sound of wagon wheels floated through the open doorway, followed an instant later by the clopping of hooves. Somebody was coming.

The Kid pulled his gun and spun toward the doorway, covering the distance to it in a pair of quick strides. He looked out into the bright afternoon and visibly relaxed. Turning back to the others, he said, "It's just the gent we were expecting."

"I'm still not sure about this, either," Doc said. "I know it's the reason we came out here today in the first place, other than dropping a loop on these two, but it seems like a bad idea."

"You worry too much, Doc," the Kid said as he holstered his gun. "All the best gangs have their pictures made. Frank and Jesse, the Younger boys . . . It's history, that's what it is. History in the making."

The Kid stepped outside and called, "Over here, Mr. Langley! We're the ones who sent for you!"

Stark frowned and looked over at Pollard. He could tell that the deputy was remembering the same thing—the wagon back in Ryanville that belonged to Phineas Langley, the itinerant photographist. On the surface it was a ludicrous thought—that the Kid would arrange for the man to come out here to the hideout and take a picture of the gang—but after Stark had mulled over the idea for a few seconds, it seemed perfectly logical, given the Kid's seemingly immense ego. The youngster had virtually created himself over again in the dime-novel image he cherished, and having a picture made of his gang fit right into that.

The Kid came back in, trailed by a cadaverous figure in frock coat and top hat. Phineas Langley looked nervous at the sight of Doc and Pops holding guns, but the Kid said exuberantly, "Don't worry about that, Mr. Langley. We were just talking to these gents. The guns are to make sure there's no trouble."

"I received the note at the hotel requesting that I come out here," Langley said, "along with the partial payment for my services. Very generous, I might add. But I had no idea that I would become involved with some sort of trouble—"

"No trouble, no trouble at all," the Kid hastily assured him. "Just a gathering of some friends, and we thought it might be fun to have our picture made as if we were some sort of desperadoes." He looked at Doc and Pops. "Didn't we, boys?"

"Sure," Doc said with only a hint of reluctance in his voice. Evidently he was used to these flights of fancy by the Kid, and as long as the youngster could lead them on such profitable jobs, he and the others were willing to put up with them. Doc looked at Pops and nodded, and both men holstered their revolvers.

Stark felt a little better without those gun muzzles staring him in the face, but only a little. He and Pollard were still in bad trouble. For the time being, though, they had little choice except to play along with whatever bizarre idea the Kid came up with next.

The Kid turned to Dinah and Belle. "You ladies can change while Mr. Langley's setting up his equipment. How would that be?"

"All right, I suppose," Belle replied. "Come on, Dinah."

They disappeared behind a flimsy partition, where, Stark figured, they had already stored some extra clothes. When they reappeared a few minutes later, their range gear was gone, replaced by fancy attire: a fine beige gown for Belle, with long sleeves, a high neck, and plenty of lace around both, along with a wide-brimmed, ribbon-decorated straw hat; and a bright red, spangled saloon dress for Dinah that brazenly showed off her charms.

In the meantime the Kid and Phineas Langley had stepped outside while Doc and Pops continued to watch the prisoners with poorly concealed suspicion. The Kid came back in first, carrying Pollard's Colt, Stark's LeMat, and a Winchester that Stark recognized as his own. The Kid gave them the weapons, saying, "Don't get any ideas. They've all been unloaded. I haven't decided what to do with you gents just yet, but you might as well get in the picture with us."

There was no telling what the Kid would come up with next, Stark thought. He took the empty pistol and rifle as Langley carried in a large, bulky piece of apparatus on spindly legs. Stark recognized it as a camera with a black cloth draped over it. Langley began setting it up.

Pollard took his gun from the Kid, who said, apparently for Langley's benefit, "Here, Dan, you left this outside."

Stark slid the LeMat into its holster, then gripped the Winchester. He wished it were loaded so he could drive a handful of .44-40 slugs right through the Kid's smirk.

"All right," Langley said, "if everyone will take their places . . .?"

"Stand up and move back a step," the Kid told Pollard. He was grinning with the excitement of arranging the pose. He pulled over a small table and placed it between the chairs. An old, empty whiskey bottle was lying in a corner of the shack, and the Kid picked it up and placed it on the table, then sat down in the chair Pollard had just vacated. "Pull that barrel over here," he directed Pops.

The old swamper moved the barrel next to the chair, and the Kid told Dinah to sit on top of the barrel. He positioned Pollard closer to her and told him to draw his gun. "Look fierce," he said with a laugh.

Pops picked up another rifle and took his place behind the table. Next to him stood Belle, and at the end of the line was Doc, who crossed his arms and rested his gun so that the barrel of the pistol still pointed at Pollard, just in case. That left Stark sitting in the chair where he had been all along.

"Hold the Winchester across your chest," the Kid told him. "We want this to look authentic." He turned to the photographist and asked, "How about this, Mr. Langley? Will it be all right?"

Langley ducked under the black cloth and peered through the lens of the camera, studying the upside-down image for a moment before replying, "Yes, the arrangement is fine. Now, everyone be perfectly still." His voice was muffled by the drape. In his left hand he lifted some sort of metal pan on a stick, and Stark realized suddenly that the pan must be full of flash powder. Langley would touch it off as soon as he was ready to take the picture.

"Isn't this great?" the Kid asked gleefully. He leaned over and said in a whisper to Stark, "By the way, I think we'll just kill the two of you once this is over."

"Don't move now," cautioned Langley.

The flash powder exploded.

The brilliant light took everyone but Stark by surprise. A split second after the flash powder ignited with a *whoosh*, Stark twisted around in the chair and lunged out of it, knocking aside both the chair and the flimsy table next to it. He drove the butt of the Winchester into Doc's belly, hoping that the gambler wouldn't involuntarily pull the trigger and hit Pollard.

"Look out!" the Kid yelled.

Doc doubled over from the force of Stark's blow, and Stark's pivoted to slap the barrel of the Winchester against the gambler's head. The pistol slipped out of Doc's fingers as he staggered back against the wall.

Pollard, following Stark's lead, lashed out at the Kid with the empty gun in his hand. The Kid was trying to get up, but he crumpled as the barrel of Pollard's Colt smashed into his skull, denting his hat.

Pops was trying to draw a bead on Stark, but the quarters were too close. Belle was swatting at him, evidently too angry at what Stark had done to her husband to think of pulling the little pistol out of her purse. Stark got a hand in her midsection and shoved her back hard against the wall.

Pollard bent to reach for the Kid's gun, but Dinah was too fast for him. Howling a curse, she scooped up the empty bottle from the floor, where it had fallen when the table was overturned. She brought it crashing down on Pollard's head, shattering the glass in a million pieces.

Stark went to one knee as his fingers finally closed over the grips of Doc's fallen gun. He angled the barrel up and fired just as Pops brought his rifle to bear on Stark's burly form. The shots were so close together that they sounded like one, but Pops was jerked backward by the slug clipping his shoulder, while his bullet whined harmlessly past Stark's head to thud into the floor.

The deputy struggled with Dinah, his balance deserting him as he tried to corral the armful of female wildcat. Both of them crashed to the floor. Grimacing, Pollard swung a fist at Dinah's jaw, the blow cracking against its target and making her go limp beneath him.

Langley was yelling as he danced around and tried to protect his precious camera from flying lead. He backed into Stark and yelped, but the big man ignored the photographist, knowing he had no connection with the gang. Langley had to be just as startled by this sudden melee as anybody.

Stark wheeled toward Doc just as the gambler barreled into him, throwing him off-balance. The impact knocked Stark to the floor. Pops fired the

182

rifle again, the slug chewing up floorboard a foot from Stark's head.

"Come on!" Doc shouted to his older brother. "Let's get out of here!"

Doc was closest to the door, and he ducked outside before Stark could get a shot at him. Pops fired wildly one last time as he followed his brother, but the bullet smacked into the wall behind Stark. Again Stark triggered the gun but saw the slug knock splinters from the doorjamb as Pops darted through the opening with surprising speed and agility.

As he scrambled to his feet, Stark heard a flurry of hoofbeats outside, accompanied by Doc's hoarse shouts. Stark ran to the door and saw that Doc and Pops had vaulted astride their mounts and jerked loose the reins of the other horses, including Stark's Appaloosa and Pollard's chestnut. All the animals were scattering, and Doc and Pops were riding hell-bent for leather through the clouds of dust outside the shack. Stark threw a couple of shots after them without much hope of hitting anything. The pounding hoofbeats never slowed or even faltered, and he knew his shots had missed.

"Damn it!" Stark said fervently. He turned back to the interior of the abandoned roadhouse and saw that Pollard had things under control. The Kid's pistol was in Pollard's hand, and the deputy had it pointing in the general direction of Belle and Dinah, who seemed to be stunned. The Kid was still out cold, sprawled on the floor.

Pollard threw a grin in Stark's direction. "At least we got three of them," he said, nudging the Kid's body with a booted toe. "Including this vicious little son of a bitch."

Langley was still gasping from shock, but he managed to say, "My God, what's going on here?"

"I'm a deputy U.S. marshal," Pollard told him, "and these folks are under arrest for robbery and murder."

"But . . . but what about that photograph I just took?"

"Develop it," Stark told him grimly. "The Kid wanted a souvenir of his gang. He's going to get one . . . before he hangs."

Chapter Thirteen

Despite being stampeded along with the other horses when Doc and Pops fled, the Appaloosa and the chestnut hadn't gone far. Stark found them a quarter-mile down the trail and brought them back to the abandoned roadhouse while Pollard was tying up Belle, Dinah, and the Kid. He stepped into the doorway just as Pollard was finishing.

"Wish I had a set of handcuffs," Pollard said as he stepped back from the Kid and surveyed his handiwork. "That rope'll have to do until we get him back to Ryanville."

The Kid was awake now, having regained consciousness while Stark was gone. He snarled up at Pollard, "You'll never get me to Ryanville, you bastard! Doc and Pops'll be back to get me!"

Stark laughed harshly. "Didn't you ever hear the old saying about no honor among thieves? The way those two lit out of here, I don't reckon they'll stop until they get to Canada."

"They'll be back," the Kid vowed. "You'll see."

Stark glanced at the women, who managed to look angry and crestfallen at the same time. A swollen bruise had appeared on Dinah's jaw where Pollard had clouted her during the fight.

Stark wished he knew just how close Doc and Belle were. Even if Doc and Pops wouldn't return to try to free the Kid, Stark couldn't imagine a man riding off and leaving his wife in the hands of the law. Still, he didn't really know Doc Teague. The gambler might be able to forget about Belle and never look back.

Reaching down, Stark caught hold of the Kid's arm and hauled the younger man effortlessly to his feet. "Come on," he said grimly. "We'll load you and the women in Langley's wagon and take you back that way."

The photographist had already loaded his camera into the wagon, and now he stood by, mopping nervous sweat from his face with a silk handkerchief. As Stark and Pollard marched the prisoners out of the shack, Stark kept an eye on the surrounding hills. Doc and Pops could have doubled back and might be up there fixing to ambush them even now.

No shots rang out, though. After the Kid and the two women had climbed into the back of the enclosed vehicle, Stark shut the lower half of the Dutch door at the rear of the wagon, securing the open upper half to the wagon's side with a hook to keep the door from swinging around while the wagon was moving. "You take the lead," he said to Pollard. "I'll ride drag where I can watch these three."

Pollard sent the chestnut trotting down the trail toward Ryanville as Langley climbed onto the wagon seat and took up the reins. Stark fell in behind.

He could see Belle and Dinah leaning sullenly against the sideboards of the vehicle. The Kid sat across from them, his face set in stubborn, angry lines. If there was any fear in him, it wasn't readily apparent.

"You'll be sorry you ever crossed me, Stark," he called through the opening at the back of the wagon. "I don't know why you threw in with that no-good lawman, but you'll regret it."

"Only thing I regret is that we didn't dab a loop on the other two of you," Stark told him. "But I reckon we can look for them again once you're behind bars."

"What've you got against me?" demanded the Kid. "I thought we were friends."

Stark took a deep breath. Maybe it would be better just to explain. Then the Kid would understand why he couldn't look to Earl Stark for mercy. "Remember the stagecoach you held up between Whitehorse and Buffalo Flat a while back? The one that turned over?"

"Sure, I remember," the Kid said. "We made a damn good haul, thanks to a pard of mine."

Stark continued, "The driver and the shotgun guard on that coach were friends of mine, good men, both of 'em. And there was a woman killed in the crash, too. She broke her neck when the stagecoach wrecked."

"Your ma, right?" sneered the Kid.

Stark shook his head. "Nope. The woman I

was going to ask to marry me when she got to Buffalo Flat."

The Kid fell silent and leaned back against his side of the wagon to glare at Stark as they rode along. Stark wanted to ask him what he had meant about a partner in the stagecoach holdup, but he could tell from the Kid's demeanor that he wouldn't get any answers.

The little caravan arrived in Ryanville not long after dark. They drew immediate attention, since the prisoners were visible through the opening at the rear of the wagon and passersby on the boardwalks recognized Belle, Dinah, and the Kid.

One man hurried out into the street to stalk along beside Stark. "What the hell's going on here?" he demanded.

"This is law business, mister," Stark told him bluntly. There was no need to keep any secrets now. "That fella up ahead is a deputy United States marshal, and I'm giving him a hand. The folks in the wagon are under arrest. We don't want any interference." One of Stark's worries during the ride back to Ryanville had been that the citizens might be upset to see three of their own in such trouble.

"Under arrest? Miss Belle and Miss Dinah? You're crazy, mister!"

Stark's right hand rested casually on the butt of the LeMat, which he'd reloaded and replaced in its holster. "I don't think so," he said heavily.

188

"You got some place around here we can use as a temporary jail?"

With no sheriff or marshal in Ryanville, there was likely no jail, either. The man who was hurrying along beside the Appaloosa shook his head in response to Stark's question, but a small crowd was tagging along now, and one of them called out, "There's a smokehouse down the street that's got a good heavy door on it. You could put a lock on it, I'd wager."

Stark turned his head and nodded his thanks to the man. "Smokehouse up ahead, Pollard," he called to the deputy.

"I see it," Pollard replied. "Drive along there, Langley."

The still-shaky photographist complied with the order, bringing the wagon to a stop in front of a squat building with thick log walls. The door, which stood open at the moment, was made of heavy planks nailed together in a double layer. Stark and Pollard dismounted, and Stark opened the bottom half of the wagon's Dutch door while Pollard stood by, his gun drawn.

"Climb on out of there," Stark told the prisoners.

The women came out first, and for a moment Stark thought he was going to have to reach in and haul the Kid out bodily. He was about to do that—and he wouldn't have been any too gentle—when the Kid emerged awkwardly and grudgingly from the wagon. Stark and Pollard prodded them at gunpoint into the smokehouse.

The crowd had grown large by now. A slender, silver-haired man in a suit came up to Stark and snapped, "See here! That's my smokehouse, and I want to know what you're doing, locking those people up in it!"

"Just like you said, we're locking these folks up," Stark said dryly. "Who're you, mister?"

"My name's Halliburton. I own the Red Top Café. And what gives you the right—"

"This," Pollard said, holding up a badge that caught the light coming from a nearby building. "I'm a deputy U.S. marshal, and these people are my prisoners. They're part of a gang that's been holding up stages and banks all over the territory."

"That's absurd!" protested Halliburton. "I know Miss Belle. She and her husband are respectable business owners . . . well, as respectable as saloonkeepers can be, I suppose. And that young man who works at the livery stable . . . why, he's just a boy!"

From inside the smokehouse the Kid said, "Thanks for sticking up for us, Mr. Halliburton. These two gents are insane—"

"No, they're not." The words came from Phineas Langley, surprising Stark a little. He had figured the photographist would want to stay out of this controversy. "I heard enough during their capture to know that Mr. Stark and Mr. Pollard are telling the truth."

Another man in the crowd called, "And we're supposed to take the word of some travelin'

190

picturetaker?" The scorn in his voice was plain to hear.

"It's the truth," insisted Langley.

"And I've got the papers to prove who I am," added Pollard.

Halliburton turned to Stark. "And what about you?"

"I'm just giving Deputy Pollard a hand. Name's Earl Stark. They used to call me Big Earl."

The name struck a note of recognition with some of the crowd. One man said, "You used to be a shotgun guard, didn't you?"

"That's right," Stark said.

"Heard tell you'd given that up and gone to lawyerin'."

"That's right, too. But that bunch of outlaws led by the Kid was responsible for the death of somebody close to me, and I gave up my practice for the time being to track them down. That's the gospel, folks, and if you've got a telegraph here, you can wire Sheriff Pete Bishop over in Buffalo Flat. He'll confirm my story."

"There's no telegraph here," Halliburton said with a shake of his head. He went on grudgingly, "But I don't reckon anybody would make up a crazy story like that. I guess we can give you the benefit of the doubt for now."

"Thanks," Stark grunted. "Anybody got a lock we can use on this door?"

Someone fetched a lock from the hardware store, and Stark snapped it in place on the hasp

191

after pushing the heavy door shut. Dinah let loose a string of curses, but Belle and the Kid suffered their imprisonment in silence.

"We'd best take turns keeping an eye on this place," Pollard said quietly to Stark as the crowd broke.

Stark nodded. "That's just what I was thinking."

They settled the matter quickly. Pollard would take the first watch, and Stark would return later in the night with his greener to stand guard. Leaving Pollard at the smokehouse, Stark took the Appaloosa and the chestnut down to the livery stable. Since the Kid was locked up, no one was there to help him unsaddle the horses, rub them down, and give them grain and water. When he had finished, he walked tiredly up the street to the hotel.

The few people in the hotel lobby gave Stark interested looks as he went up the stairs to his room. This was probably the most excitement to hit Ryanville in a long time, Stark thought. He hoped it was over, though. All that remained to be done now was to transfer the prisoners to the authorities, which meant taking them all the way to Buffalo Flat, where they could be turned over to Sheriff Bishop and locked up in his jail to await trial.

When Stark reached his room, he took off his hat, duster, boots, and gun belt, then sprawled out on the bed in the rest of his clothes. Weariness spread through him, weariness and a peculiar empty feeling. He had expected to feel better once he'd caught up with the gang. But Laura was still dead, and there was still a hole inside him where he felt the loss.

He rolled onto his side and tried to sleep, but tired as he was, a long time passed before he dozed off.

The internal alarm that frontier life instilled in a man who wanted to stay alive woke Stark a few hours later, around midnight. He stood up and stretched, then sat down again to pull his boots on. After a few minutes he walked out of the Moffatt Hotel, wearing his hat, his duster, and the LeMat and carrying his shotgun tucked under his left arm.

This end of the street was dark and quiet, but a lot of noise was coming from the smaller saloons at the other end of town. Stark stayed alert as he walked toward the smokehouse. The doors of the Ace-High were closed, the lights blown out, the piano stilled. Somebody else would take over the saloon, Stark imagined, and it wouldn't be long before things were back to normal in Ryanville.

He wished it would be that easy for him.

"That you, Big Earl?" Pollard called as Stark approached.

"It's me," replied Stark. Pollard stepped out from the deep shadows at the side of the smokehouse, and Stark asked him, "Any trouble?"

"Not a bit. Halliburton came back and talked to me for a while, and I convinced him we were

193

telling the truth. He was pretty upset that he and the other folks in town were taken in by the gang for so long. Said the rest of the citizens would be, too."

Stark frowned slightly. "Don't much like the sound of that. Folks who feel they've been made fools of sometimes take some pretty rash actions. I don't want anybody talking themselves into forming a lynch mob."

Pollard looked up the street to where the other saloons were still roaring. "I don't want that kind of trouble, either. That's why I think we'd better move these prisoners first thing in the morning."

Stark looked around and asked, "What happened to Langley's wagon?"

"He drove off in it," Pollard replied. "I don't know if he planned to stay around or not. He was still pretty shook up by everything that happened. Said it was a miracle none of those bullets flying around smashed his camera."

"Well, I reckon we couldn't very well ask him to loan us his wagon again, anyway. We'll have to rent one to take the prisoners to Buffalo Flat. There's a good strong jail there where they can be held until they stand trial."

Pollard gave Stark a shrewd look in the moonlight. "After what that bunch did, I'm a little surprised you don't want to string them up yourself," he commented.

"I thought about it," Stark admitted heavily. "I've got to try to follow the law, though. I swore an oath, just like you did."

"Glad to hear you say that. I didn't really want to go up against you again." Pollard rubbed the back of his neck. "I'm about done in. I'm going to get some sleep. Be back in about four hours."

"I'll be here," Stark told him.

Pollard walked off toward the hotel as Stark moved into the shadows to take up guard duty. He listened to the sounds floating down the street from the saloons that were still open, and he didn't like what he heard. The voices were loud and raucous, but not particularly happy. There wasn't much laughter, and what there was had an ugly tone to it. For long months Ryanville had nursed a nest of vipers in its bosom, and now that the citizens of the town knew what had happened, they were angry about it.

Stark decided he would be damned glad when he and Pollard and the prisoners had put Ryanville behind them.

A few minutes later a hissing sound from inside the building caught his attention. Listening closer, he realized it was the Kid whispering his name. Stark went to the front of the smokehouse and put his mouth close to one of the small gaps around the door. "What the hell do you want?" he asked in a low voice.

"Look, Stark, you're only going to get yourself killed if you keep on being stubborn like this," the Kid whispered back. "I tell you, Doc and Pops are going to come back for me, and they'll kill you for sure, maybe a lot of innocent people, too."

195

"What do you want me to do, let you out?" Stark asked with heavy irony.

"You could, you know. It stinks to high heaven in here, what with all these hams hangin' up, and there's not much air. Besides, no matter what you do to me, it won't bring that lady friend of yours back."

"You'd better shut up about her," Stark grated.

"All right, all right, take it easy. Listen to me, Stark. I know where there's plenty of money. I cached the loot from our jobs, and Doc and Pops don't know where it is. That's why they'll be coming for me."

Stark frowned. If the Kid was telling the truth, that would be a powerful motive for the two members of the gang still at large to try to rescue him. Doc and Pops wouldn't get their share of the loot if the Kid was in jail, or worse, strung up at the end of a rope.

"What are you saying—that if I let you out of there you'll split the money with me?"

"That's right, Stark. Take it from me, money'll make you feel a lot better than revenge. I know that from experience."

Stark wasn't interested in the Kid's story. In fact, he was trembling with such rage that it was all he could do not to throw open the door of the smokehouse and let the Kid have both barrels of the greener. If the Kid thought he could bribe away Stark's grief and anger with stolen loot, then something was missing inside the Kid's head,

Stark realized suddenly, some piece that told a man the difference between right and wrong.

That didn't change the Kid's guilt, though, not one damned bit. And Stark didn't feel any sorrier for him than he would have for a mad dog. The Kid needed to be put down just the same way.

"You'd better think about it," the Kid prodded. "These bitches are sound asleep, so you could let me out and leave them here for Pollard."

"Shut up," Stark said flatly. "Shut up or I'll give you to that mob that's trying to drink themselves some courage down the street."

The Kid chuckled. "You wouldn't do that, Big Earl."

"Don't be so damned sure." With that, Stark went back to his spot beside the smokehouse, hoping the Kid would keep quiet. Stark didn't know how much more he could take.

A couple of hours passed slowly. The noise from the saloons continued, but when no mob appeared, Stark began to think that the town's anger had peaked without any violence and would now begin to die away. He was glad, because he honestly did not know what he would have done if a crowd bent on lynching the Kid had appeared at the makeshift jail. Legally, of course, the Kid—along with Belle and Dinah—had to stand trial. But in the end he would be hanged anyway, a part of Stark's brain insisted. A lynching tonight, in Ryanville, would be premature justice, but the

197

result would be the same. The Kid would dance on air, just as he deserved.

Stark drew in a deep breath and let it out in a sigh, the questions still circling endlessly inside his head.

Suddenly he spotted a figure approaching the smokehouse. He lifted the greener and warned, "You'd better sing out, mister."

Dan Pollard's voice came back. "It's me, Stark. I was having trouble sleeping, so I thought I might as well come back down here and keep you company."

Stark lowered the greener and said, "I was restless myself. Come ahead."

He stepped out to meet Pollard in front of the smokehouse and quickly told him what the Kid had said about the hidden loot. "If it's true, we'll have to worry about Doc Teague and Pops all the way to Buffalo Flat," Stark concluded.

Pollard grimly agreed. "You're right. They won't let that money just slip away—"

A sudden commotion made both men turn and look down the street. Men were spilling out of the open saloons, and angry shouts filled the night air. Somebody yelled, "There's a rope on that hoss! Grab it!"

"Son of a bitch!" Pollard said under his breath. "I was—"

"So was I," Stark said. "But like it or not, here they come."

Chapter Fourteen

The burly lawyer and the deputy marshal moved to stand shoulder to shoulder as the mob approached, their shouts loud and filled with rage. Stark hooked his thumb over the double hammers of the greener but didn't cock it just yet. Indecision still lurked in his mind. But he would back Pollard's play anyway. The deputy deserved that much.

"We've come for the Kid!" one of the men shouted as the crowd came to a stop in front of the smokehouse. "You gents stand aside!"

"You know I can't do that," Pollard said, quietly but firmly. "There's not going to be any lynching. You men go on back to your homes."

"He played us all for fools!" someone else cried. "When this story gets out, Ryanville's going to be the laughingstock of the whole territory."

"Better that than being known as the town where a man was lynched," Pollard said, his voice a little louder now. "Ryanville may be isolated, but it's part of a civilized society. There's law and order here."

"What law and order?" The question was shouted back at him. A man pushed to the front of the mob and went on, "My daughter-in-law was killed when that bunch robbed the bank in Dover City and rode out shootin'! Who knows how many other folks they killed?"

"I say there's not going to be any lynching, and by God, I mean it!" responded Pollard, and his voice was an angry roar now. "What sort of men are you? Are you planning to string up those two women, too?"

"No, but they can sure as hell watch while the Kid swings!" snapped one of the mob's ring-leaders. "What about you, Stark? It's all over town how the Kid's gang killed your woman. You goin' to stand for that?"

So this was it, Stark thought. The time to either take a stand or back down, to follow his emotions or the law.

"I stand with Deputy Pollard," he said. It was damned near the hardest thing he'd ever done.

"Then you can fall with him, too, you son of a bitch!"

The mob surged forward, too full of whiskey courage to think about the guns they were facing. Stark hesitated, and so did Pollard. Both men knew that these were honest citizens attacking them, not outlaws.

And that hesitation was just enough to make the difference.

Hands grabbed the barrels of Stark's greener and wrested it away from him before he could fire. Fists slammed into him, knocking him back against the wall of the smokehouse. Shouts of rage filled the night air, blending with frightened screams from inside the smokehouse as Belle and Dinah, awakened by the commotion when the mob approached, feared for their lives in this frenzy of violence. Pollard slashed with his gun barrel at the heads of the men nearest him, but somebody slammed the stock of a rifle over his head, knocking his hat off and sending him to his knees.

Stark fought back as best he could, but he and Pollard were heavily outnumbered. He felt himself going down under the weight of the mob, and as he was borne to the ground, more fists and booted feet crashed into him. The world began spinning crazily around him.

With a great shout he heaved himself to his feet, throwing off the hands that tried to hold him down. Before he could do more than swing a couple of long, looping punches at the crowd surrounding him, however, something slammed into the back of his head and sent him pitching forward. This time when he fell he was unable to get up. The night turned red, then faded to black as more blows fell on him.

Stark never completely lost consciousness. After the blows and kicks stopped thudding into him, he lay there in the street, breath rasping in his throat, and listened as someone in the mob used the butt of a rifle to smash the padlock and hasp on the door of the smokehouse. The shouts rose in volume and intensity as the door was pulled open and the prisoners were dragged out. Stark heard the women screaming again and the

Kid cursing in a high-pitched voice, but there was nothing he could do. His muscles wouldn't obey the urgent commands his brain was sending for him to get up and put a stop to this.

Anyway, he was tired, and his head hurt, and Laura was still dead, so what the hell was the point? He lay there as the sound of the mob moved away down the street.

They were still yelling when Stark let out a groan and lifted his head. Somebody had lit some torches, and the hellish glare revealed the scene at the other end of the street to Stark's bleary eyes. Men were struggling to get the Kid on the back of a skittish horse, and nearby other members of the mob were tossing a lariat over a branch of an oak tree that shaded the town well. Off to the side, more men held Belle and Dinah, who writhed in their grips and looked on, horror-struck.

Stark twisted his head and saw Pollard lying on the ground a few feet away. The deputy's hat had been knocked off, and there was blood on his head. He was breathing, though; the street was lit well enough for Stark to see Pollard's chest rising and falling. Pollard was just knocked out cold.

Stark pushed himself to his hands and knees. He stayed that way for a minute, dragging air into his lungs and blowing it out while the pain in his head subsided a little. He spotted his greener a few feet away, lying unfired where it had fallen during the struggle. Carefully he reached out and wrapped his fingers around the stock, pulled the shotgun to him, and then used it to brace himself as he climbed unsteadily to his feet.

Stark checked the LeMat. It was still in its holster. He left it there for the time being as he began to stagger down the street. If anyone had asked him, he couldn't have said if he was going to try once more to put a stop to the lynching . . . or just looking for a better view. But he kept walking, his pace steadying as he neared the frenzied cluster of men.

The mob had the Kid on the horse now, his hands tied behind him. They held him on the animal's back while a couple of other men tried to slip a noose over his head. The Kid wasn't cooperating, though, twisting back and forth and writhing around in the grip of the men holding him on the horse. He wasn't going to make it easy for them.

Stark lifted the greener, his finger going through the trigger guard in readiness.

Somebody punched the Kid in the stomach, causing him to freeze in pain long enough for the rope to be jerked over his head. The noose was pulled taut.

Stark opened his mouth to yell for the mob to stand back, but at that instant two riders swept around a nearby corner on horseback, galloping their mounts straight at the mob and firing wildly with the six-guns in their hands. Doc Teague and Pops let out savage howls as they attacked the mob in a last-minute effort to save their partner from the lynch rope.

Stark wheeled toward the two outlaws and touched off both barrels of the greener. Flame and smoke belched from the double barrels as the gun boomed. The twin charge of buckshot whistled through the torch-lit street and sent Doc's horse tumbling to the ground. The gambler flew over the horse's head and landed heavily, rolling over and over. Pops sagged in his saddle, blood on his duster where the buckshot had wounded him, but he managed to turn his pistol toward Stark and squeeze off a shot.

Like the slap of a giant hand, the slug clipped the outside of Stark's upper left arm, the impact knocking him halfway around. He dropped the greener and put down his left hand to catch his balance as he fell to one knee, ignoring the pain that spread up and down his arm. With his right hand he palmed out the LeMat.

Doc was back on his feet, staggering a little but still dangerous. He fired twice, the bullets whipping past Stark. Stark snapped a return shot with the LeMat and threw himself to the side, rolling behind a water trough at the side of the street.

The mob was scattering as the lead flew. They had been brave enough to string up a man with his hands tied behind his back, and they had even swallowed enough bottled courage to overwhelm Stark and Pollard at the smokehouse. But this gunfight between Stark and the outlaws was different. A stray bullet could cut down anybody.

Still on horseback with the noose around his neck, the Kid had been deserted by his would-be executioners. The horse was moving skittishly, spooked by all the gunfire, and as he swayed desperately in the saddle, trying to stay upright, the Kid screamed, "Get me down from here! Goddammit, somebody get me down!"

Stark lifted himself enough to throw another shot at Doc, who was scurrying toward cover on the opposite side of the street. Pops veered his horse toward the Kid, but suddenly a shot rang out from down the street, and the outlaw's horse went down. Pops kicked his feet free of the stirrups and threw himself clear of the falling animal in time to keep from being crushed by it. The old man scrambled to his feet and darted toward a wagon parked nearby, moving with an agility that belied his age and his wounds.

Stark looked down the street and saw Pollard running toward the fracas, smoke still curling from the barrel of the pistol in his hand. The deputy had fired the shot that took down Pop's horse, Stark realized. But across the street, Doc was drawing a bead on the approaching lawman.

"Get down, Pollard!" Stark shouted as he fired at Doc to distract him. The bullet thudded into the rain barrel behind which Doc was crouched, and water began to spout out through the hole.

"Somebody help me!" shrieked the Kid. The horse under him was lunging around more and more, and the Kid was holding tight to it with his knees, leaning far to the side to keep some slack in the rope as he tried to control the horse.

Pollard ducked into the mouth of an alley and used the corner of a building for cover as he threw a shot at Doc. Stark had to turn his attention to Pops, who was on the same side of the street as he was, using the parked wagon for cover. Pops fired, the bullet smacking into the end of the water trough behind which Stark crouched. He was going to have to hunt for better cover, Stark realized, because the water trough wasn't going to offer him any protection from Pops.

He rolled over and surged up onto the boardwalk. Another slug kicked up splinters from the planks at his feet as he threw himself toward a recessed doorway in the building. There were windows all around the door and the little alcove wasn't going to provide much shelter for him, but it was better than nothing. Glass shattered over his head as he knelt there, and he bit off a curse as he realized that he had left himself open to Doc's fire once again.

They had him between a rock and a hard place.

"Help!" yelled the Kid hoarsely. "Oh, God . . ."

Stark fired and put another hole in Doc's rain barrel, and more water poured out. The water level in the barrel had to be dropping, and Stark knew the water was what was stopping his bullets from penetrating. If he aimed at the upper part of the barrel . . .

Doc didn't give him a chance. The gambler

squeezed off three shots at Stark, forcing him to throw himself down flat in the doorway. From the corner of his eye Stark saw Pops race out from behind the wagon and head for the Kid, taking advantage of Stark's being pinned down.

Pollard must have had the same idea as Stark about the water in the rain barrel, because his gun blasted twice, and Stark saw the slugs smack through the top section of the barrel. Doc gave a harsh cry and rolled out from behind it, clutching a shattered left shoulder.

Stark pushed himself to his feet. Pops had almost reached the Kid, and the light from the torches dropped by the fleeing mob shone off the blade of the knife in Pop's left hand. He was going to cut the bonds on the Kid's wrists, thereby freeing him to get the noose off his neck.

If that happened, Stark knew, the Kid would gallop out of town without looking back, and Stark might never catch up to him again.

Stark launched into a stumbling run, weariness gripping every muscle in his body. His left arm was on fire from the bullet crease, and his heart was pounding heavily in his chest. But he wasn't going to let anything stop him. He wasn't going to let the Kid escape.

"Hold it, Pops!" he shouted.

Pops was only a few feet away from the Kid now, but Stark's challenge forced him to stop and turn, bringing up the revolver he still held in his right hand. Flame geysered from its muzzle as he fired.

Stark heard the bullet sing past his ear as he pulled the trigger of the LeMat. The bullet punched into the old outlaw's chest, driving him back against the horse on which the Kid squirmed frantically. Pops stumbled forward, trying to center his gun on Stark and fire again, but Stark fired the LeMat twice more before Pops could get off a shot. The bullets spun him around, and he crumpled in the street, almost under the hooves of the crazed horse.

"No!" the Kid screamed, feeling the horse shifting under him.

The animal was about to bolt, and this time the Kid would never be able to control it. Without thinking, Stark ran forward, reaching up to grab the animal's halter. He hauled down on the reins, bringing the horse under control.

There were two more gunshots behind him, so close together they sounded almost like one. Stark turned to see Pollard and Doc facing each other. Doc had somehow made it to his feet and tried one last time to down Pollard, but it was the lawman's bullet that had gone home. Doc swayed for a second, then plunged forward on his face, dead before he hit the ground.

"Reckon it's over," Stark said heavily.

"Son of a bitch," muttered the Kid. "I thought I was a goner for sure."

Stark's head snapped up. The Kid was pale and shaken, but some of the arrogant self-confidence that had been in his eyes earlier was already starting to reappear. Stark said, "You were right, they came back for you. But it was almost too late."

"I expected better of 'em. I'll have to find me some better partners next time."

"Next time?" Stark repeated bitterly.

"Sure," said the Kid. "You don't really expect me to hang or go to prison, do you, Stark? I'll get away somehow. You lawmen just don't understand. Desperadoes like me lead a charmed life." The Kid grinned, enjoying listening to himself talk now that the danger was over. "Think about it. Tonight I almost got lynched, but you saved me. I knew you couldn't stand by and watch them hang me, Big Earl. Hell, you're a lawyer, I hear tell. You do things proper."

Stark dragged in a deep breath and looked up at the Kid, seeing the unrepentant evil in his eyes and remembering Laura Delaney. He sighed heavily and said, "That's right, Kid. Got to see that things are done proper."

Stark turned away. But as he did, he brought his hand down in a sharp slap on the horse's rump.

The Kid had just enough time to let out a startled cry as the horse lunged out from under him. His eyes widened in the stunned realization that he had finally pushed Stark too far, and then the noose bit into his throat. His weight hit the end of the rope, and there was a snap as his neck broke cleanly.

Justice had caught up to the Kid, and it was a

better end than he had deserved, Stark thought as he walked away without looking back.

He became aware that someone was yelling at him and looked up to see Pollard, livid, saying, "You bastard! You killed him!"

"Somebody needed to," Stark said flatly.

"You're just as bad as them," Pollard said, waving a hand at the townspeople, who were beginning to emerge from their hiding places now that all the gunplay was over.

Stark didn't feel like arguing, but he didn't see it that way. The citizens of Ryanville had tried to lynch the Kid out of their stubborn, offended pride. With Stark, pride had nothing to do with it. All he had done was wipe out an evil, the same evil that had taken Laura from him, the evil that would have killed more innocent people if given half a chance. Try as he might, he couldn't see anything wrong with that.

He shouldered past Pollard, saying, "I reckon you can arrest me if you want to."

Pollard hesitated, then said, "No. I'm not going to arrest you. But you're going to have to live the rest of your life with what you've done, Stark."

That was fair enough, Stark supposed. He limped on into the night, bone tired, never looking back at the figure dangling at the end of the rope.

Pollard didn't even glance in Stark's direction as he drove past in a rented wagon the next morning on his way out of town with the remaining prisoners. Stark stood on the board-walk in front of the café, weary but feeling almost human again. He had cleaned the bullet crease on his arm the night before and bandaged it as best he could, then fallen into an exhausted but restless sleep. His arm was stiff and sore this morning, but he was able to use it and was getting around fairly well. A plate of bacon, five eggs, half a dozen biscuits, and a pot of coffee at the Red Top had made him feel even better.

Now Pollard was leaving Ryanville, taking Belle and Dinah along with him. Stark knew from the conversations he had overheard around town this morning that the two women had tried to escape in the confusion of the previous night, but with their hands tied, Pollard had quickly run them to ground. The bodies of the Kid, Doc Teague, and Pops were at the undertaker's, waiting to be planted in the local potter's field before the day was over. Nobody was going to mourn them.

The whole town was still buzzing about what had happened, and listening to the talk, Stark had learned something else interesting. Nobody seemed to realize that he was the one responsible for the Kid's hanging. The story going around was that the horse had spooked and bolted during the fighting. With all the bullets that had been flying, the townspeople had all had their heads down at the crucial moment. Belle and Dinah had already taken off at that point, so they didn't know any better, either. From the looks of it, only Stark and Pollard knew the truth of what had happened.

Stark didn't bother correcting the false impression. In the cold light of day, he was still convinced he had done the right thing, but he wasn't particularly proud of it. Pollard had been right; Stark was going to have to live with the knowledge that for one moment he had allowed the spirit of vengeance to overtake him completely. Maybe that was a bad thing . . . and maybe it wasn't. The whole idea of vengeance and justice sometimes got as muddied up as a shallow stream after a whole herd of cattle had crossed it.

Stark stood there and watched the wagon carrying Pollard, Belle, and Dinah out of Ryanville. Pollard's chestnut was tied on behind the vehicle. Stark wished that things hadn't ended this way between him and Pollard. The deputy was a good man.

"Mr. Stark?"

Turning on the boardwalk, Stark saw Phineas Langley walking toward him. The tall, slender photographist had something in his hand, and as Langley drew nearer, Stark saw that he held a picture. Langley extended it toward him.

"I developed that plate, just as you asked, Mr. Stark. Here's the print."

Stark took it and looked at the figures posed there. Belle and Dinah had broad smiles on their faces, while the Kid, Doc, and Pops all looked stern. Stark and Pollard were grim-faced in the photograph, but anyone looking at it would never have guessed that they weren't part of the gang. It had turned out just as the Kid wanted.

A bunch of desperadoes and their women. Right out of a dime novel.

Stark looked up at Langley. "What do I owe you?"

The photographist shook his head and said, "I've already been paid, remember? Even though the Kid promised me more, what he gave me was sufficient."

Stark nodded. "All right. But can you make another print from that plate?"

"Well, I suppose so. It will look the same as that copy, though."

"That's what I want." Quickly, Stark ripped the photograph he held in his hand, ignoring Langley's gasp of surprise. He tore the picture so that the Kid was separated from the rest of them, then slipped that part of the photograph into the pocket of his vest.

No one in Ryanville seemed to know the Kid's real name or where he was from or if he had any family. But one of these days, Stark mused, he would find out. He wanted to let the Kid's family know what had happened to him—and he was curious about the home life that had spawned such a cold and ruthless killer. All Stark knew for sure was that he couldn't quite let go of this, not just yet. He was going to keep on worrying at it, like a dog with a bone.

"I'll . . . get that other photograph made for you," Langley said somewhat uncertainly. "No charge except for the chemicals and the paper."

"Thanks," Stark said. "How long will it take?"

"It should be ready before the day is over."

"Good. I'll be back for it before I ride for home."

But Stark knew he had one more thing to do, one more question to be answered, before this was really over.

Chapter Fifteen

The ride back to Buffalo Flat was a long one, made even longer by the memories riding with Stark: memories of Laura Delaney and the violence he had encountered in tracking down her killers, memories of an almost-friendship with Dan Pollard, memories of the Kid and the rest of the gang, immortalized in the photograph carried in his saddlebag.

And memories of something that the Kid had said, back there in Ryanville.

As the miles rolled past under the hooves of the Appaloosa, Stark thought about everything that had happened since the day he had ridden out to meet the stagecoach carrying Laura from Whitehorse. He tried to recall everything he had seen and heard, and he knew the answer that had come to him was the right one.

He couldn't do anything about it until he got back to Buffalo Flat, though, so he pushed the Appaloosa fairly hard, anxious to write an end to the story at last.

Finally Stark left the Maricopa hills behind him and hit the stage road between Buffalo Flat and Whitehorse. As he passed the spot where the holdup had taken place, he felt a twinge deep inside, a mixture of sorrow and regret. The burning urge for revenge was gone now, but its loss had not affected the other feelings. Only time was going to do that, Stark sensed.

As he rode, he also considered what to do about his law practice. Was he fit to be a lawyer after what he had done to the Kid? True, no one other than Pollard knew about that, but *he* knew. That was enough.

Giving up his practice wouldn't accomplish a damned thing, though, and Stark knew that as well. As a lawyer he could do some real good, he was sure of it. And maybe one day, through the efforts of lawyers and doctors and teachers and lawmen like Dan Pollard, the West would be tamed enough so that human wolves like the Kid wouldn't have a place anymore. Stark was going to hold on to that hope.

When the buildings of Buffalo Flat came into view, Stark kept the Appaloosa at a trot until he reached the main street, where he slowed the big horse to a walk. Some of the townspeople on the boardwalks saw him and called out greetings, which Stark returned with a wave of his free hand. He wasn't in the mood to talk to anybody just yet.

But when Judge Tobias Buchanan and Sheriff Pete Bishop came striding out into the street to greet him, Stark had no choice but to rein in and swing down from the Appaloosa. They were his friends, and he was glad to see them.

"Good to have you back, Earl!" Bishop said

as he caught Stark's hand and pumped it. "Did you catch up to those bandits?"

Judge Buchanan shook Stark's hand, too, and said to the sheriff, "Let the poor man catch his breath, Pete. Can't you see he's had a long ride?"

"Thanks, Judge," Stark said. He was aware of the crowd gathering around him and wished that folks would back off for the time being. He didn't want an audience when he told the sheriff and the judge what had happened over in Ryanville.

Bishop took his arm. "Come on over to the Tumbling Dice. I'll buy you a drink."

"In a few minutes, Pete," Stark told him. "There's something I've got to do first."

"All right, but we'll be waiting for you." Bishop turned to the onlookers. "Break it up, folks. Nothing to see here. Bud, you take Mr. Stark's horse over to the livery and see that it's tended to."

Stark was grateful for that. He made his way through the dispersing crowd, putting up with the slaps on the back from citizens welcoming him home, and turned his steps toward the stage line office. He had to see Martin Suggins right away.

Suggins had heard the commotion heralding Stark's return to town and stepped out onto the porch to see what was going on. He grinned broadly as Stark approached. "Hello, Earl," he called. "I was afraid we'd never see you again."

"There was a time or two I didn't know if I'd

make it back myself, Martin. Reckon I can talk to you for a few minutes?"

The smile on Suggins's face disappeared as he recognized the seriousness of Stark's expression. "Sure, come on into the office," he said. "If you don't mind me saying so, you look like hell warmed over, Earl."

"Feel like it, too," Stark said as he followed Suggins into the building. No one else was in the office at the moment. The hostlers were all in the barn out back, Stark supposed.

Suggins went behind the waist-high counter that ran across the room and leaned his palms on it. "What is it, Earl? Did you find any of the gang that was holding up my coaches?"

"Found all of 'em," Stark replied. From the reactions of the townspeople, he had already guessed that Pollard hadn't brought Belle and Dinah here after all. The deputy had probably turned south at the stage road and headed for Whitehorse instead. A railroad station was there, and Pollard could have taken the prisoners all the way back to his headquarters. That would explain why no one in Buffalo Flat knew what had happened.

Seeing the anxious expression on Suggins's narrow features, Stark went on, "Most of them are dead now, and the ones who aren't are in custody."

"Did you . . . did you happen to recover any of the money that was stolen?"

Stark shook his head. "Nope. It was stashed

somewhere, and the secret of the location died with the gang's ringleader. I'm afraid that loot's gone for good, Martin . . . except for the share that *you* got, of course."

Suggins stared at him. He licked his lips, which seemed to have gone dry. "I . . . I don't know what you're talking about, Earl."

"Talking about the share that the Kid sent to you for tipping the gang off every time there was something really worth stealing on one of your coaches," Stark said. "The Kid admitted he had a silent partner, and there's nobody else it could be except you. You were robbing your own stage line. Reckon when you had enough socked away, you'd have closed up shop here and said that you were quitting because of all the robberies. Then you could have taken the money to start a new life somewhere else." Stark shook his head. "Don't really know why you'd want to do such a thing. Seems to me you had a pretty good life here. Just greedy, I guess. That's the downfall of most men, sooner or later."

His eyes wide with shock, Suggins managed to shake his head. "This . . . this is crazy! You don't mean any of this, Earl. We were friends—"

"Used to be," Stark agreed sadly.

"You can't prove it. You can't prove any of it—"

"The Kid told me." It was a bluff, but one Stark was willing to risk. "He thought he had me dead to rights, and you know how the Kid liked to brag. He told me all about being partners with you, Suggins."

The face of the stage line owner suddenly contorted with hatred and fear. "You'll never tell anybody else!" he exclaimed shakily. "I'll kill you! I'll say you went crazy mad with grief—"

His hand dropped below the counter, reaching for the gun Stark knew was there.

Stark wasn't particularly fast on the draw, but he was faster than Suggins. The would-be killer's gun was barely above the level of the counter when Stark's LeMat roared and planted a.42 caliber slug in his shoulder. Suggins screamed as he was thrown back by the impact of the bullet. Stark stepped around the counter and kicked the little pistol Suggins had dropped out of reach.

Staring down at Suggins over the barrel of the LeMat, Stark said, "There was a time I would've killed you for your part in all this, Martin, but I reckon it'll be enough to see you go to jail. I maybe forgot about it for a while, but I *am* still a lawyer. We'll let the law handle it from here on out."

Suggins just moaned and writhed, clutching his bloody, shattered shoulder.

Pete Bishop pounded into the room, gun drawn, and slid to a startled stop when he saw Stark standing over Suggins. "Earl! What the hell's going on here?"

"Come on in, Pete. You'd better send somebody for the doc first, though. I don't want ol' Suggins here to bleed to death, not before he stands trial." Stark holstered his gun. "I'll tell you the whole story, and then we'll go get that drink." He took a deep breath. "I could use it about now."

Chapter Sixteen

Stark, Bishop, and Judge Buchanan sat by themselves at a table in the rear of the Tumbling Dice, talking in low voices as Stark explained everything that had happened since he had left Buffalo Flat to pursue Laura's killers. He told the truth, including what had really happened to the Kid, knowing that he could trust the sheriff and the judge. The story didn't reflect particularly well on him, he thought, but he had never been one to lie to friends.

When he was through, Bishop blew out his breath noisily and said, "I'm glad Ryanville's not in my jurisdiction, Earl. I'd hate to have to make up my mind what to do about you."

"Sounds to me like you just carried out the sentence any judge would have passed, had the case come to trial," growled Buchanan.

"Then you don't think I ought to give up my law practice, Judge?" asked Stark.

"Give up your law practice? Good God, man, what are you thinking? The West *needs* good honest lawyers. Don't let a possible—and I emphasize *possible*—lapse of judgment force you to abandon your career!"

"Well, that's what I was thinking, too," Stark said with a slight smile.

"We're with you, Earl," Bishop told him with a grin and a nod.

The conversation made Stark feel a little better about things, and now he leaned back in his chair and sipped from the mug of beer in front of him. His attention was drawn to the front of the room, where a man in shirtsleeves, vest, and string tie had just entered. The newcomer looked around the room, then lifted a hand when his gaze fell on Stark. He started toward the back of the room.

"Jehoshaphat," Stark muttered. "What now?"

He had recognized the newcomer as Merle Goodrich, Buffalo Flat's telegrapher, and he saw that Goodrich had a yellow telegraph flimsy in one hand. As the man came up to the table, he said, "There you are, Mr. Stark. I heard you got back into town, and I've got a wire here I've been holdin' for you nigh onto a week now. Here you go."

Stark frowned as he reached to take the telegram Goodrich held out to him. Who in blazes could be sending a wire to him? Stark moved the message back and forth for a second, then gave up and dug out the pair of reading spectacles from an inside pocket. He settled them on his nose and scanned the words Goodrich had printed on the paper.

The message was simple, if mysterious. It was a request for Stark to travel to Washington City, District of Columbia, at his earliest convenience for a meeting with the man who had signed the wire—the attorney general of the United States.

"What the hell?" Stark exclaimed fervently.

"Let me see that," Judge Buchanan commanded. He took the telegram from Stark and read it quickly. "So you're going to Washington City, eh?"

"But what for?"

Buchanan put the wire on the table and tapped it with a blunt finger. "This doesn't say, but I assume it's something important if you're being summoned clear across the country."

Stark's eyes narrowed abruptly with suspicion. "You sure you don't know anything about this, Judge?"

"Not a thing, my boy. You have my word on that."

Stark leaned back in his chair again. "Well, I don't know if I'm going or not."

"Not going?" Bishop said. "Hell, Earl, you've *got* to go. It ain't every day a man gets sent for by the attorney general of the whole blessed United States. How can you not go?"

"Well," Stark muttered, "I reckon I ought to. I suppose it wouldn't hurt to find out what it's all about."

"That's the spirit. Besides, after all you've been through, I think a trip will do you good." Judge Buchanan picked up his glass of beer. "Here's to Earl Stark . . . and whatever destiny awaits him in Washington City."

Stark had never seen such a place in all his days. Washington City was big enough that a dozen Buffalo Flats could have been dropped down into its boundaries and still not fill them up. And so many people were in the streets and the buildings that it reminded Stark of some anthills he had seen. Everybody hurried here and there at a pace that made him tired just to watch.

He had sent a wire to Washington City to let Augustus Garland, the attorney general, know that he was coming, then started packing. The trip east had been surprisingly quick once he reached Whitehorse by stage and boarded a train. The iron horse had made the country a lot smaller than it had been less than a quarter of a century earlier. Stark had seen a lot of pretty scenery during the journey, but now that he was actually in Washington City, he felt uneasy. He longed for some open range instead of buildings and cobblestone streets everywhere he looked.

An aide to Attorney General Garland met him at the train station, saw that his gear was loaded into a waiting carriage, and took him to the building that housed the offices of the Justice Department. Garland greeted him effusively, saying that he had heard about all his exploits out West.

"Exploits?" Stark echoed.

"There'll be time to talk about all that later," Garland said. "We took the liberty of booking a room for your stay at the finest hotel in the city, compliments of the Justice Department. My carriage will take you there once we're through."

Stark nodded and said, "Much obliged."

The attorney general consulted his watch. "Well, we'd best be leaving if we don't want to be late. We don't want to keep the President waiting."

Stark swallowed hard and managed to say, "No, sir, we sure don't."

The carriage was waiting outside the Justice Department. Stark and Garland climbed aboard, and the driver sent his team trotting briskly down the Washington City streets until it reached Pennsylvania Avenue and drew up in front of the White House. Stark stared at the presidential mansion as he climbed out of the carriage, blinking in disbelief. He had read about the White House in newspapers and books, but he had sure as blazes never figured to be visiting it.

The whole thing was a little like riding a bucking bronc, Stark thought—scary as all hell, but you didn't want to get off before it was time. The attorney general ushered him past the guards and into the White House, where President Grover Cleveland was waiting for them in a room more opulent than anything Stark had ever seen in the fanciest hotel. Stark shook hands with the tall, bulky, distinguished-looking man, who smiled and said, "We've certainly heard a great deal about you, Mr. Stark. You cut an impressive figure, to say the least."

Stark wouldn't have gone that far—he supposed he looked all right in the store-bought suit Judge Buchanan had helped him pick out— but he couldn't very well contradict the

226

President. He said, "Thank you, sir. I'm mighty impressed and pleased to be here."

"The pleasure is all ours," the President assured him. "And I know you're going to do great things for us."

"Sir?" Stark couldn't keep the bafflement out of his voice.

Cleveland looked over at the attorney general. "Mr. Stark *has* been informed why he's here, hasn't he?"

Garland inclined his head slightly. "I assumed so, sir, but if that's not the case, perhaps you'd care to . . .?"

"Of course." The President laughed heartily and went on, "Mr. Stark, if you care to accept the offer, you've just been appointed a federal circuit court judge."

"Son of a—" Stark caught himself just in time as he blinked at the startling news. "A federal judge, you say?"

"That's right," Garland told him. "If you accept the post, you'll be covering a far-flung circuit through the Western territory, dispensing law and justice wherever you're needed. Are you interested in the position, Mr. Stark?"

"But . . . I've only been a lawyer for a few months."

"Perhaps, but we've been assured of your qualifications for this post," President Cleveland said. "There's no need to hide your light under a bushel, Mr. Stark. We know that you have one of the keenest legal minds to come along in recent years."

Someone had been spinning some tall tales, Stark thought, and for the life of him, he couldn't figure out who it might have been. But one thing cut through clearly in the confusion that had his mind swirling: He had just been offered a judge-ship, a post that was an incredible honor for a frontier lawyer. The more he thought about it, however, the more sense it made. The West had its own special legal problems, and who better to sort them out than a judge who knew the land and the people? Maybe this was a good idea after all.

Suddenly an image of the Kid at the end of a lynch rope flashed through his brain. He asked himself if he had any right even to be here in the White House, let alone to accept a job as a circuit judge.

The answer was clear. If he could do some good, he had to at least try. And it was true he knew the law as well as or better than most of the other lawyers west of the Mississippi.

He looked the President in the eye and said, "I'm honored to accept the offer, sir. And I'll do the best job I can."

"I know you will, Mr. Stark." The President looked and sounded relieved for some reason, and so did the attorney general. Both of them shook hands with Stark again.

"You'll be sworn in tomorrow, Mr. Stark,"

Garland told him. "Or perhaps I should just go ahead and say Judge Stark."

Judge Stark, the former shotgun guard thought to himself. It had a strange sound to it, but a good one.

When all the handshaking and congratulating was over, Garland again offered to have the carriage take Stark to his hotel. Stark nodded his thanks, then shook hands one last time with the two high officials and left the White House.

Pausing on the sidewalk outside the White House gate, Stark drew a deep breath and blew it out. This trip back East had been full of surprises, that was for sure.

And they weren't over yet, he discovered a moment later. He heard a voice calling his name, a voice that was somehow familiar, and turned to see a slender, well-dressed man striding toward him, smiling arrogantly.

"Hello, Stark," Representative Cassius P. Hamilton said. "You're a long way from home, aren't you?"

Stark stiffened with dislike. "How the devil did you know I was here, Hamilton?" he demanded.

"How did I know?" The legislator's smug smile widened. "Why, it's because of me that you *are* here, Stark. *I* proposed that you be offered that federal judgeship and called in enough favors to see that it got done. It wasn't too hard, actually. There weren't that many candidates interested in the vacant position, since the circuit involved is in the West."

This was all going too fast for Stark to keep up with. He shook his head and said, "I just don't understand—"

"Do you know what the life expectancy is for judges out West, Stark?" Hamilton asked. "Why, you'll be gunned down by some irate litigant or frustrated barrister before you've spent six months on the bench. And I'll have the satisfaction of knowing that it was through my efforts you met such an inglorious end!" He leaned closer to Stark and hissed, "You never should have made a fool of me that day in Buffalo Flat!"

Now Stark understood. Hamilton had made it plain. Stark met his hostile glare for a few seconds, then stepped over to the curb where the carriage with his gear was waiting to take him to the hotel. He opened the door and reached inside, under the overcoat he had brought with him. When he turned around, the short-barreled greener was in his hands, and Hamilton suddenly found himself staring in horror down the twin bores of the weapon. Stark deliberately left the weapon uncocked, but Hamilton never noticed that.

"Six months, eh?" Stark said as he smiled grimly at Hamilton over the double barrels of the scattergun, ignoring the shouts of the bystanders and their scurrying to get out of the way in case of violence. "Well, we'll just see about that. I got a hunch the West hasn't seen many judges like me. Now git!"

Hamilton didn't even think about trying to beat

a dignified retreat in the face of the greener. He turned and ran like a rabbit, realizing to his dismay that Stark might indeed be correct.

Epilogue

". . . And so as I look out at this assemblage of esteemed colleagues, friends, and family, I want to conclude that I am a lucky man indeed. For I have known the best of both worlds, from the rough-and-tumble of stagecoach days to the corridors of power in our nation's capital. I have been allowed to wield the weapons of law and order ranging from the sawed-off greener of the shotgun guard to the law books of the practicing attorney to the gavel of the frontier jurist. It is my humble, fervent prayer that I have been fair and proper in my dealings with all of them. I am honored to have been here today. Thank you, and good afternoon.

"Oh, one more thing, if I may. If any of you boys want to come on over to the barroom after all this folderol's done with, the first round's on me . . . Wait a minute! Is that newspaper fella still writin' down what I'm sayin'? Hold on there! I want to have a word with you, mister—"

BRAWL AT LAWYERS' CONVENTION; ESTEEMED JURIST CHARGED IN FRACAS.
—Headline from the Denver Post, August 2, 1895